Dark Pools of Light

Iris Clyde

Inca Publications

Dark Pools of Light

ISBN 978-0-9558681-1-5

Published by Inca Publications
Voresheed
Berstane Road
Kirkwall, Orkney
KW15 1SZ

A CIP catalogue record of this book can be obtained from the British Library.

Book designed by Michael Walsh at
The Better Book Company Ltd

and printed by
Ashford Colour Press
Unit 600 Fareham Reach
Fareham Road
Gosport
Hants PO13 0FW

Cover photo by Martin Findlay

For my sons

Also by the same author:

Shimmering Waves and Dancing Shadows

1

The stars were fading into the pale sky of early morning and the gravel was white with hoary frost when Jocelyn set off on her journey north. It was late March but the weather was still wintry, with a fine dusting of snow veiling the grass along the verges and clinging unevenly to the barks of the trees and their spreading dormant branches. She wound down her window and took several deep breaths, the cold air stimulating her sluggish brain and energising her body, after a restless night of whirling macabre dreams and indecision; but that was behind her now. She adjusted her speed to the road conditions, driving slowly along deserted roads and through sleepy villages, her rotating tyres marking her progress. As the sun grew warmer, the snow melted away, and the comradeship of a smile and a casual wave from another early starter was gradually replaced by the introverted expressions of workers, following a familiar route as part of their daily routine.

She joined the motorway at the first opportunity and stopped at a service station to fill up and buy a map. She also bought a book of coloured photographs, with breathtaking shots of the North Highlands and Islands. It was large and cumbersome to prop up and peruse while she ate breakfast at the café, but it focused her mind, blotting out the past and firing her enthusiasm for the trip ahead.

There was one photograph of Trowsay, the island to which she was heading. The shot had been taken from the sea looking into a cave, where the undulations of the waves within, cast uneven light on a circle of misshapen rocks. The caption to this photograph read: "There is a myth that when the sea is high and the moon is in the right position to shine into the cave, the moving waves and the shimmering light make the shadows of the rock stacks dance against the uneven surface of the back wall like a troop of trows (or trolls) planning their mischief." She studied the photograph closely, wondering if it had been touched up to give credence to the story. Even if it had, it still needed a good bit of imagination to see what was described.

Once back on the road, she made better speed, driving up through the industrial heart of Scotland, to the Highlands and eventually to the narrow, desolate road wending northwards through mostly grey, barren land to the Kyle of Tongue and the Atlantic Ocean.

Now that she was nearly at her destination, she was forced to face the reality of her situation. The advert had invited artists to 'write for details' and she had not written. She had planned to say: "I was coming this way anyway and thought I'd call in". From a distance, and cocooned within the embracing familiarity of her car, that had seemed a reasonable excuse for not writing; but now, in exposed isolation, sitting at a rust-streaked table on the terrace of the Talhaugh Hotel, looking across the rushing waves to the island of Trowsay, it sounded false. She could see that this was not the sort of place where one found oneself without purpose.

She gnawed at the side of a nail that had already been bitten to the quick and sank her neck into the turned up collar of her Barbour. The east wind was light but it was straight off the sea and biting cold; the low wall provided no shelter. The landlord had said that it was too cold to sit outside, but the empty, dark bar with its acrid smell of stale beer and tobacco smoke had determined her choice.

She reached forward to her plate and lifted the dry edge of a roll that she had left uneaten and sucked it unconsciously as she thought about the advert in *The Artists' Review.* It had read: "A comfortable home offered to three travelling artists who have reached the end of the road", and was written in script on an artist's palette in the shape of the island, with three tiny figures in artists' garb, clutching easels and tottering on its rim. In geographic terms, of course, Trowsay was 'at the end of the road', and the bizarreness of the advertisement could merely be a way of attracting attention and thus custom, but the ambiguity of the last phrase had resonated with her. She had cut it out (burning the magazine so that Bill would not see the scissored space) and kept it safe.

She got up and sat awkwardly on the stone coping of the terrace with the wind on her face. It fluttered her cap of glossy black hair and gave reason for the moisture in her eyes. She could hear the sea splashing against the cliffs below and watched the resultant mesmerising swirls of spume being consumed by the next incoming wave. Along the west coast of the island, massive slabs of rock jutted and bit into the shoreline, embracing and then discarding the regular torrents of seawater. The browns of the cliffs and the greens of the land reflected the dullness of the day.

There was a caravan on a headland to the east where the sea rippled on a sandy beach but there was no sign of any houses. It was a bleak and uninviting scene. She could still go back, she reminded herself. The postcard she had written to Bill when she stopped for lunch (addressed to his onshore base so that he would not get it until he returned to work in a week's time) had said that she had decided to take her mother on holiday. A wave of cold sickness churned inside her. She did not want to go back.

As she watched, with growing depression, a man came round the eastern headland and started to amble down the cliff path. She took her binoculars out of her pocket and focused on him. He stopped walking and gave a loud, sharp whistle. She had not seen a dog and scanned the shore and the heath land above. There it was, leaping through the long grasses and heather after a bounding hare. The dog was a short-legged breed and it was no match; it soon gave up the chase and started back down the hill, disappearing and reappearing with each jump over the rough-stalked heather. It reached the path and looked up at its master with panting breath and wagging tail, before leading the way down the cliffside. At the shore, the man lowered himself on to a large boulder and opened a tobacco tin that he had been carrying. He rested it on his knee and started to roll a cigarette. It was quite a performance getting it to just the right thickness and length. Once he was satisfied, he settled it in his mouth and struck a match. His dog was playing with the waves, barking when he mistimed his retreat and was caught by a rush of water. Something caused the dog to stop playing and start growling. The man got up, his cigarette stuck to his lip, and walked over to see what there was to see. The water oozed round the soles of his boots and over his toes as he bent to lift something up. He turned it over in his hand, rubbing the surface in thought, and then threw it away with a long sweeping movement. She could not see if the object of interest was the bone of a dead animal or something artificial which had been lost or discarded, but she watched it flying through the air and plop into the sea. When she refocused on the shore, the man was looking straight at her. She lowered her binoculars, ashamed to be caught spying, and waved in apology. He waved back and went on waving, smiling and beckoning to her. The dog started dancing about, yelping and wagging its tail.

Her depression lifted. It was an irresistible invitation.

She paid her bill and went back to her car.

The island of Trowsay was joined to the mainland by a raised road supported by massive concrete blocks and, as she drove across the narrow tarred surface, she caught only brief glimpses of the sea through the irregular peaks of grey concrete. There was no sign of the man or his dog. Her disappointment turned to shock when he rose from behind the last block and his dog rushed at the car, barking and biting at the tyres. She stopped quickly, fearful that she might have caused it harm.

"Is he all right?" she called out in concern from her opening window.

"Dinna read a'thing into Heidi's attack," the man said, lifting his greasy bonnet in greeting and exposing a shiny, milk-white head, which contrasted with the ripe colour of his veined face and bulbous nose. He propped his arm on her roof, his lipless mouth parting to show an even white smile. "She doesna care for Rover cars."

"Why is that?"

"It's him we don't care for," was the enigmatic response.

The man was very old, his faded blue eyes resting on folds of loose skin, with deep crevices running from cheek to chin. "Apologise to the lady now, Heidi," he went on, leaning down and scooping his dog up. The dachshund reached through the open window and licked her cheek. It would have leapt into the car if it had not been held tightly.

"What a beautiful dog!" she exclaimed, smiling into the dog's liquid brown eyes and stroking her silky ears. She could see that it was a pure breed; the man and the dog made an odd pair.

"Aye she's a rare treasure," he replied with pride, settling the dog down on the road and half-straightening up, his inquisitive face close to hers. "You winna be daeing the island justice looking round at this time o the day. It'll be dark within the hour."

"I was going to call in at a house called Atlanticscape," she told him, reaching for her map.

"So you were efter a bed?"

"Perhaps."

"It's a queer lot of folk living there noo. Some o them any road."

That was not what she wanted to hear, but before she could respond and enquire about alternative accommodation, he had straightened and turned away from her, his attention redirected. She could hear the revving of a powerful engine as a vehicle approached the crossing and changed down a gear. Looking back through her mirror, she could see that it was a red sports car with its roof down; the driver was resting his elbow casually on the window frame and she had a fleeting impression of blonde hair, ruffled by the wind, and rugged features.

"Here's Thorfinn," the man said, giving a wave. "He's biding there the noo and will see you right." He stood on the other carriageway, blocking the road, so that the car was forced to a stop.

The driver greeted him and responded to Heidi's clawing of his door by reaching over and lifting the dog on to his knee. He sat back, restraining the dog's exuberance, and smiled at Jocelyn with genuine warmth. He also appraised her openly, adding a low whistle of admiration, which had the effect of tinting her translucent skin with colour. She raised her head in a haughty gesture and lowered her cool green eyes, widely spaced below delicate eyebrows. Her response was meant to be a rebuff but when she lifted her lashes, she saw that he was only amused.

"The lady here's on her way to Atlanticscape," the old man told him, sealing her fate. "I was just saying that you'll lead the way for her."

"A pleasure." The words were said with a broad grin. "Hi, there. I'm Thorfinn Dukes."

She extended her hand through her open window and murmured: "Jocelyn Fenwick."

"You'll be one of Phil's artists."

She bit the side of her lip not knowing how to reply to that.

"Well... "

The old man leaned forward and clutched her hand. "I'm Davey Petersen," he said, keeping himself in the thick of things. "You didna say you were one o they artist types." The heat was throbbing up through the veins in his face. "I may have spoken out of turn a while back.

They're not a' queer mind, just some."

Thorfinn's face crinkled into a wide-mouthed smile, his deep-set eyes nearly disappearing. He lifted Heidi off his knee and put her back down on the road. "Davey had his portrait painted," he said to her in explanation, "and it wasn't to his liking."

"It was nae portrait," Davey responded without humour. "A right mess it was. I would only hae looked like that if the knackers' van had carted me off and run into the nearest wall."

She commiserated and assured him that she was a traditional artist.

"He'll be getting you to paint his portrait next," Thorfinn warned.

"You couldna make a worse job of it, that's for sure."

Thorfinn gave a chuckle before letting out his clutch. "See you around, Davey," he said in farewell, his salute changing to a beckoning gesture, indicating to Jocelyn that she should follow him. "Onwards and homewards."

Davey was reluctant to let her go. "I'm nae saying that you wouldna make a grand job o'it mind."

"I know you're not," Jocelyn said quickly, starting her engine.

"I'd be happy to pose for a lovely lass like you."

"Thank you." She smiled quickly up at him before letting out the clutch and pressing the accelerator. She would have liked to have made her departure less abrupt but she did not want to lose the sports car which was travelling at speed up the slope ahead. When she looked back through her rear window, she saw that the old man had not taken offence. He was watching her, his shoulders pulled back and his thumb hitched in the armpit of his aged jacket in a stately pose. His dog had risen to the occasion and was sitting up straight beside his parted feet. She smiled to herself at the incongruous picture they made, knowing that if she were still around, she had committed herself to painting them like that.

The car in front stopped at the top of the incline and Thorfinn came back to speak to her. "Atlanticscape is to the right here," he said. "You follow the main road to the end, go through the village and up past the harbour. The sign for the house is on the gate pillar."

"I thought you were going that way."

"I am, but I want to take a quick run up to the Selkie Bay farmhouse first." He must have noted her dismay because he went on: "If you are not in a hurry and would like to come....?"

Jocelyn dithered.

"You will be quite safe, I assure you,"Thorfinn teased. "My Hanna is there and will keep me in order." His flirtatious words were softened by an ironic smile.

"I'll stay with you," she murmured, a flush suffusing her cheeks. She would have rather continued on her journey, but she did not want to lose the protection of her escort; someone to support her and introduce her when she arrived at her destination.

They took the alternate turning and travelled along a straight road for about a mile with reed beds and a large inland loch to her right and undulating farm land to the left. The breeze was whipping up the surface of the loch, which was grey and uninviting, reflecting the overcast sky. At the far side of the loch, she could see a large mansion house, three storeys high with turrets and pillared portico. It seemed incongruous in the bleak landscape.

Ahead of her, Thorfinn was slowing. He looked over his shoulder and pointed to a house up on the hill. She could see that it had originally been a traditional stone-roofed cottage with a door in the middle and windows either side, but the door had been glazed and a large extension was rising at the rear, covered with banks of scaffolding. Thorfinn started up the track, avoiding the roughly repaired potholes in the disintegrating road; she followed him with more care, driving into a courtyard, packed with cars, a fork-lift truck and a cement mixer. The half-built extension joined the old house to a farm building, which was in a poor condition, with a sagging roof and missing slates, exposing the beams beneath.

Thorfinn gave a loud peep on his horn and a woman came out of the extension to greet him with a wide smile and open arms. She was tall and slender, dressed in stained jeans and a loose man's dress shirt, torn at the side.

"A good journey?" she asked, lifting her face to be kissed.

"It's always a good journey on the way home," was Thorfinn's response, as he gave her a tight squeeze and another kiss. "Come and meet one of Phil's artists who has just arrived." He put his arm around her back and brought her across to be introduced.

"Hallo," she said giving her name and shaking Jocelyn's hand with a welcoming smile. She had deep-blue eyes, with soft hollows beneath her cheekbones and thick honey-coloured hair, falling in loose waves to her shoulders. "Phil didn't say he had an artist arriving today."

Jocelyn looked shame-faced as she introduced herself, giving her prepared excuse about being in the area. It sounded false. Her easel and other painting paraphernalia could be seen with her luggage on the back seat of the car. "I'm afraid I've left it very late in the day," she went on, feeling foolish "I should have written first."

Hanna regarded her pensively.

"Don't worry now," Thorfinn said quickly, to counteract Hanna's reserve, "Phil is very easy-going and won't send you away without a bed for the night."

Hanna agreed with that, before turning to survey the courtyard. "You're going to have difficulty in turning."

"We'll back up," Thorfinn told her. "Will you be long?"

"I'm nearly finished. Just wait while I speak to Mike and then we can be on our way."

Thorfinn squeezed her hand and watched her go.

"It might be best if you waited at the bottom, he suggested to Jocelyn. "I've got to get Hanna out." He indicated a Range Rover immediately ahead of her.

Jocelyn nodded. She was feeling sick with anxiety as she turned her car, going back and forward on Thorfinn's directions. It was only early evening but the light was beginning to fade and Hanna's shock at hearing that she was not expected at Atlanticscape had made her feel even worse about her situation. She made up her mind to return to the Talhaugh Hotel for the night and waited at the bottom of the track, with her engine running, to tell Thorfinn that; but the minutes passed and there was no sign of him. She turned her engine off and laid her arms along the top of the steering wheel, resting her forehead and closing her eyes, trying to blot out her anxieties.

Thorfinn forestalled her words of excuse by calling out, as he spun his car round and came to a stop beside her: "I gave old Phil a ring and he's setting another place at table. He's a great guy. Makes fun furniture."

Relief overwhelmed Jocelyn and her eyes filled with tears. "Thank you," she whispered, turning to get her handkerchief out of her handbag.

"Don't get upset now. It'll be o.k. You'll see."

She blew her nose. "I should have written first."

"It's not a problem. Hanna is just very protective of Phil, that's all." He got out of his car and started to pull up the hood. "It's getting a bit chilly now."

Jocelyn thought that it had been chilly for the last few hours and said so.

"You'll get used to our spring weather being extended winter."

"There was frost on the ground when I left home and there had been snow in the night."

"You see! We get better weather up here."

She changed the subject by pointing across the loch to the pseudo castle standing high above the water, and asked him about it.

"Trowsay House,"Thorfinn told her, glancing towards it briefly as he secured his hood. "It was privately owned until the mid-eighties, with only an elderly man and his housekeeper rattling around in it, but it's a hotel now and the only pub on the island."

"It's incredible to see such a building on this small island."

"That's how the wealthy Victorians lived. They had big families. Ah, here's Hanna now." He gave her a wave and invited Jocelyn to follow him, manipulating his long body into the low seat of his car. He started his engine and called out of his window: "It's a good eight miles from here but there will be a roaring fire to warm us when we get there." .

They retraced their initial route at speed, Jocelyn's car sandwiched between the other two vehicles. Davey was waiting at the junction, standing back in the long-grassed verge, holding his dog's collar, but Jocelyn had little time to acknowledge him before they started along the other side of the loch. She had to keep up, although it made her anxious to travel at such a pace on an unfenced, strange road with ewes and lambs grazing along its edge. They circled the Trowsay House hotel and Jocelyn found herself right at the edge of a rocky bay; the house had either been built there or the sea was gradually encroaching. She got a shock and nearly stalled her engine when a wave crashed against the cliff edge and spiralled upwards as she passed, spray falling on the road right behind her. A moment earlier and her car would have received the deluge. Hanna slowed down but the next wave did not have the same force and she soon made up with them as they continued north along the main road, with moor and rising heath on one side and fenced fields on the other. They reached a T junction at the top of a village with an open view of the sea, enclosed by high cliffs. Jocelyn looked about her but she had barely time to take note of the vista of houses built round the harbour with fishing boats moving at their moorings, before Thorfinn drove down the slope, past the slipway and up the other side to the Atlanticscape gates. It was now quite dark and the long driveway up to the house was in a poor condition. Thorfinn's speed slowed as he moved from side to side, trying to pick out the potholes in his headlights. Jocelyn followed him, avoiding most of the deep, ragged hollows but occasionally feeling the bump and splash of collected rain water.

The house did not come into view until they had topped the last incline. It was large and square with a single storey wing at the back, and was completely covered with dormant, entwining branches of Virginia creeper. The outside light was on, shining out brightly on the gravelled forecourt, and a large hefty man stood in the doorway. He lumbered down the steps and came towards her, waving and calling a greeting to Thorfinn and Hanna as they drove past; they turned in through an archway at the end of the house which, Jocelyn assumed, would lead to the garages.

Her first impression of her host was that he was late middle-aged, with gentle eyes, thick bushy eyebrows and wiry grey hair; his generous smile lifted the bags of loose flesh around his jowls.

"Welcome to Atlanticscape," he said, introducing himself and opening her door to help her out.

"I'm sorry for arriving like this," Jocelyn began, shaking his hand and giving her name before rushing into her prepared explanation for arriving without prior notice, but she was quickly interrupted and told that it was of no consequence and that there was always a spare room for visitors.

"We can see how it all pans out," he went on, turning to greet Hanna as she approached them from the archway. He put a friendly arm across her shoulders and asked about her day.

"I'll tell you at dinner," she said, smiling up at him. "I just wanted to make sure that Jocelyn was all right."

"I'll look after her. Off you go now."

"We'll meet up later, Jocelyn. OK?"

Jocelyn thanked her extravagantly and waved to Thorfinn who was standing beside the arch, waiting for Hanna to return. She assumed that they had their own flat somewhere round the back of the house.

"Let me get your case," Phil offered, opening the back door of the car and surveying the heap of miscellaneous belongings that had been packed in a hurry. "We'll leave most of your luggage until tomorrow unless there is anything perishable."

"Just the odd yoghurt and half-eaten sandwich and that can wait until I tidy everything out," Jocelyn said. She indicated the suitcase she needed, apologising for it being a bit heavy.

"No problem." Phil assured her, manipulating the case out. "I'm not in great shape now but I was a weightlifter in my younger days." She looked at him sideways as they walked to the front door and could see that he had the bulky frame of a man who had been well muscled at one time. "I am always promising myself that I will take a bit more exercise."

"Aren't we all," she said with a smile.

Phil closed the front door behind them and Jocelyn was stopped in her tracks by the extraordinary décor of the walls and ceiling between the outside and inner doors. The porch light shown upwards to a translucent rainbow and a wonderland of characters from nursery rhymes and children's classics: figures could be seen climbing ladders, up and over the rainbow, or flying above it and casting shadows on the ceiling. (Peter Pan, Wendy and Tinkerbelle) They all appeared to be interacting with each other although they were from different historical times. On the wall there were deeply carved plaques and a mirror that had been inspired by the wicked, vain queen in Snow White and the Seven Dwarfs.

"This is entrancing!" she exclaimed, clasping her hands and peering at the nearest plaques, which gave words to the figures cavorting above.

"It is my childish pleasure to welcome visitors in this way," Phil said, pleased that she liked what he had done.

"Thorfinn said that you made fun furniture but this is quite exceptional."

"I'm glad you like it." He opened the inside door. "Come, I'll take you to your room on the first floor. If you stay with us," he went on, "you will have a top floor studio room." He gestured to the balustrade on the top floor. "We never really got round to doing much up there and it is pretty basic, I'm afraid, but you can paint the walls and do anything you like to stamp your personality on your room."

"I hadn't expected anything quite like this," Jocelyn said in amazement, as she followed him up the wide carpeted staircase. The carved oak banisters encircled a stairwell and there was a large rose window in the domed ceiling far above, the divisions and colours of its leaded panes copied in the pattern and colours of the tiles in the hall below. "Have you many artists staying?"

"Just two at the moment. You'll meet them when you come down for dinner. We did have three but Benjie left at the end of last week."

Jocelyn wondered why Benjie had left but did not want to ask in case the reason would rekindle her doubts. She wanted to stay.

"Here we are," Phil said, crossing the first floor landing

and opening one of the panelled doors. He led her in, lifting her case and laying it across the arms of an upholstered chair. The room was large and carpeted in a golden yellow, with twin beds and a basin in the corner. The two long windows had floral curtains, falling from gathered pelmets to touch the floor; they had been drawn against the black oblongs of night. It was cosy and warm with the faint smell of new paintwork.

"This is truly lovely," Jocelyn said, turning a full circle as she inspected the room. She took both Phil's hands in hers and thanked him again for his kindness.

"Hanna helped me with the décor," Phil said gruffly, deflecting her fulsome praise. "She knows more about that sort of thing."

"I shall thank her when I see her."

"You will see her at dinner. We meet in the parlour off the front hall for drinks between six-thirty and seven."

Jocelyn only unpacked her sponge bag and night things. It seemed to be tempting providence to take the rest of her clothes out of her case and put them away. All had gone well so far, but she still had to meet the rest of the household.

She took off her travel stained clothes and washed, wondering what to wear. Meeting for drinks before dinner sounded formal, requiring more than just a change of jeans. She extracted her only good dress from half way down her case and shook out the creases. It was a fine wool, predominantly turquoise but with a small geometric pattern in shades of blue and green which combined and separated into different shapes and colours when she swung her hips. It had a mandarin collar and flared out from a matching belt.

Once she was dressed and ready, she sat watching the hands of her alarm clock move forward until it was exactly a quarter to seven. She felt nervous about entering the quaintly-called parlour on her own, but when she glanced over the banister, she saw Phil waiting for her in the hall below

"I hope I'm not late," she said, as she descended the stairs.

"Not at all." He gave her his hand as she reached the bottom step. "Come into the parlour and let me introduce you to everyone," he invited, guiding her towards a partly open door ahead of them and ushering her in. A golden retriever immediately sprang up from his prone position beside a wheelchair and welcomed her, with wagging tail and raised head, demanding petting.

Her first impression was of a large bright fire in a modestly proportioned room, made extraordinary by the richness of the over-lapping oriental rugs and the paintings that covered the walls from the light oak frieze at waist height to the ceiling cornice. The paintings were abstract; not her taste, but they made magnificent splashes of colour on the off-white walls.

"Enough now, Slavers," Phil said, giving the dog a pat on the head and accepting the brief redirection of his affections. "Jocelyn, this is my friend, Rupert Treatham." He introduced her to the emaciated man in the wheelchair. Rupert lifted a hand to hers but there was no pressure in his fingers. "And this is Bridget who specialises in stained glass." A light-skinned woman in a red sari held out her hand without moving her position. She was wide and fleshy, taking up more than her fair share of the sofa, and her streaked, artificially-red hair was raised and entwined into a robust chignon. "And Jason." Phil indicated a shy young man hiding behind thick-lensed spectacles and falling hair, blotched with green paint. He was sitting on a chair positioned against the back wall and looked awkward when he got up, leaning forward to shake her hand without moving his feet, and remaining standing, as if he didn't quite know what to do with himself.

"Sit here beside Rupert," Phil suggested, "and I'll pour you a drink. What will you have? We just have wines or beer."

Jocelyn settled for a sherry and sat down where Phil had indicated.

There were drinks and glasses on a silver tray close by and as Phil uncorked the bottle and poured her drink, he told everyone that she was an artist and had travelled far to be with them. "We must be on our best behaviour," he finished, with a soft twinkle in his eye, handing her the sherry glass.

She responded with a grateful word of thanks.

"I'll leave you to it and see what's going on in the kitchen," he said plodding towards the door. "Be good."

"And what do you paint?" Rupert asked, watching Phil leave the room. "Are you an expressionist artist like Duncan?" He indicated the paintings on the wall. "Or do you paint in some other style?" Despite his weak body and fight for breath between phrases, she could see that there was nothing wrong with the man's mental capacity.

"I like doing flower paintings," she said.

"Does Phil know that?"

"He hasn't asked."

"I'd keep quiet about it, if I were you. The love of Phil's life did these," he gestured again towards the paintings, "and he was looking for someone to carry on his tradition."

"Jason is an abstract expressionist," Bridget said languidly, "but I am not inclined towards expressionism."

Rupert looked at her balefully and said nothing.

"I make up for it by helping Phil with his work."

"You only put coloured glass in one of his carvings."

"But an important one," Bridge responded without heat. She turned to Jocelyn. "Phil was in the middle of doing 'the old woman who lived in a shoe' when I arrived and I put the glass in the windows."

"Where is Hanna?" Rupert interrupted querulously. "She should be home by now."

"She's in the kitchen," Bridget told him.

"Someone go and get her. I want her here."

Jason looked alarmed, obviously wondering if Rupert meant him, but Bridget said, without moving: "She'll come when she's ready, Rupert. Relax."

"Relax! What do you mean by relax?"

"It doesn't help you to get worked up."

"If you won't get her, I'll go and get her myself." He started moving his chair but a wheel got entangled in one of the rugs and the effort was too much for him. He sat back, his breath coming in short gasps.

"I'll get her," Jason said quickly, going towards the door and bumping into Hanna as she hurried in. This caused him to leap back as if she had attacked him. Hanna started to apologise but her attention was immediately redirected to the dog who had bounded forward and leapt up to embrace her with his paws. She responded to his warm welcome with a reciprocal hug and brushing of cheeks before walking across to kiss Rupert on the lips. "How are you tonight?" she asked.

"I'm not well at all."

Hanna smoothed his hair down, murmuring sympathetic words.

"I miss you when you're away for so long, dearest," he went on petulantly.

"I know you do, but I'm back now." She went behind his chair and pulled on the handle, releasing the wheel from its snagged position. "Dinner is ready everyone."

Jocelyn finished her sherry in one gulp and nearly choked.

"You could have taken that through," Bridget said, manipulating herself upright, and Hanna turned to apologise for hurrying her.

"A waste of good sherry," Rupert murmured.

Bridget waited until the wheelchair was well on its way before whispering: "Take no notice. He just doesn't like having us around."

"Benjie felt it," Jason blurted out, closing the parlour door behind them. "He was very sensitive to atmosphere."

"What atmosphere?" Brenda enquired sharply as they crossed the hall towards the back of the house. "Rupert has little to do with us."

Jason did not reply. He just pushed his spectacles up his nose and bent his head forward to follow the movement of his feet, his hair flopping forward. Jocelyn could feel the tension between the two of them; the first indication that living in a house of strangers with complex personalities might not give her the peace of mind she craved.

They emerged from the passage leading through from the hall into a brightly-lit kitchen, warmed by a large Aga. The room was homely rather than stylish, polished flag-stones, old armchairs and free-standing cupboards mixing with strip-lighting, ethnic rugs and white modern appliances. The central table was set for dinner and a large poached salmon lay on an ashet there, its salivating aroma making Jocelyn realise how hungry she was; it was hours since she had eaten.

Phil pulled out a chair for her next to Bridget and when they were all settled she looked round, wondering where Thorfinn was going to sit. She was about to ask when Phil forestalled her.

"Now that we're all here, I'll dish up," he said, looking directly at her, his eyes registering alarm. "Some salmon, Jocelyn?"

"Yes, please."

The relationships were confusing. Up at the farmhouse, she had witnessed Thorfinn and Hanna's open intimacy and had assumed that they were married. Hanna was wearing a wedding ring. Now she couldn't be sure what their relationship was because Hanna seemed to be involved with both Phil and the invalid Rupert. Both were of an age to be her father but neither had been introduced as such.

Bridget took the plate that Phil was holding out and dropped it quickly on Hanna's place mat. "That's hot, Phil."

"Here, let me put them down for everyone," Phil said, holding the next plate with his napkin and sliding it in front of Bridget.

She thanked him before turning to Jocelyn and saying:

"You will have the studio next to mine. I'm afraid it is the smallest one up there and with the least light."

"Let Jocelyn relax after her journey," Phil said evenly. "She will see the room tomorrow."

"But you will stay, won't you? We don't want another Benjie. He never did any work, as far as I could judge."

"He was pleasant enough," Hanna commented, cutting up Rupert's fish and mixing it with the sauce, "but we simply didn't know why he was here."

"He was lonely," Jason said quietly, not lifting his head.

"But he wasn't an artist."

"He was a conceptual artist."

"What is that?" Rupert asked.

"Dead animals hanging in formaldehyde and unmade beds," Bridget told him.

"He certainly left an unmade bed behind," Hanna said with a smile. "Thankfully no dead animals."

"Did he tell you that he was a conceptual artist?" Phil asked Jason.

Jason thought for a moment. "I asked him if that was his medium and he said yes."

"He wasn't an artist, Jason," Phil told him. "I found out after he had been here for a couple of weeks that he just wanted a bolt hole."

Bridget turned to him wide-eyed: "Bolting from what?"

"A broken relationship. His partner had been an artist and that is how he came to know about my advert." He got up and offered a little more sauce.

Bridget took some more and complimented him on his recipe.

"It's Hanna's recipe," Phil said, turning to Rupert and

asking anxiously if he wanted something else. "You've eaten nothing."

"Stop fussing," Rupert replied fretfully, followed by an enquiry directed towards Jocelyn: "Are you married?"

"Rupert!" Hanna reprimanded, laying down her fork and knife.

"Some married women go off and leave their husbands."

Jocelyn lowered her eyes. "I'm a widow."

"Now, Rupert, you know the rule."

"What rule?"

"Not to pry into anyone's circumstances," Phil said quietly but firmly. "It is an infringement of the right to privacy."

"You've always been a mother hen, Phil."

"That's enough, Rupert," Hanna said quietly but with authority. "You're being an old grouse and abusing Phil's hospitality."

Rupert's mouth turned down and he looked miserable. "You won't go off and leave me, dearest."

"I won't if you behave."

There was an embarrassing silence and it was left to Phil to break the tension: "You haven't given us a run down of your day yet, Hanna. How is the renovation work coming along?"

Jocelyn listened as Hanna told them about the problems she was having in joining the two old buildings together; they were to be a house and a restaurant. From the previous dialogue, she was now sure that Hanna was married to Rupert and she wondered how she could go on with the building work when it was clear that her husband was now terminally ill and would not live to benefit from it. In fact it was stranger than that. Where was Thorfinn. Could Hanna have started an affair with him prematurely and he did not want to face her husband in case he guessed.

No doubt she would find out all their secrets in time.

That is, if she stayed.

2

It had been nearly midday before Bill briefly touched consciousness that morning. His body was throbbing with heat and his mouth was dry and rancid; the smell of beer and cigarette smoke clung to his pillow and the air around him. He threw off the bed clothes but made no move to get up, slipping back into sleep. The next time he woke, his wet T-shirt was clinging to his body like an icy poultice and he was shivering. He pulled the duvet back over him, but its cold surface gave no warmth; there was nothing for it, but to drag himself out of bed and totter through to the bathroom, clutching the duvet closely round him. He groaned when he saw his greasy, pallid skin and red-veined eyes in the mirror and slumped down, supporting his weight on the edge of the basin while he sucked at the running cold water tap and splashed his face, over and over again. When he straightened up, with the duvet now lying in a crumpled mound round his feet, he felt a bit better; there was colour in his cheeks, and quick blinks of his eyelashes went some way to cleansing his light blue eyes. He rubbed his face dry and patted the front of his pale hair, not wanting to encourage any further hair loss with vigorous action, before turning on the jet shower for a prolonged hot and invigorating shower. Only after that, was he able to face the day.

And that meant facing Jo.

He tied a towel round and went downstairs to find her, but the house was depressingly silent and empty. She was often out in the afternoons working in the volunteer shop at the hospital or visiting friends, but he wished that she had been there so that he could have made peace with her, assuaging his guilt in her forgiveness. He knew that it had been the coward's way out to indulge in a long drinking session at the club and spend hours in front of the television set, watching a late-night movie, before going up to bed.

He drank a glass of orange juice and put the kettle on for coffee, standing at the kitchen window and looking out at the garden. The grass had grown unevenly since its last cut in the autumn and the soil in the vegetable patch was drab and uninviting but he needed to do some physical work to keep his body in shape and take his mind off his troubles. He debated about going to the gym but decided that the ground was dry enough to dig over, ready for him to put in the early potatoes next time he was home. They were laid out in boxes in the shed and had already started to sprout.

When he was ready to go back upstairs with his mug of coffee, he looked round for the newspaper. Jo usually left it on the table or on the unit beside the door but it was in neither place. He wandered through the house looking for it and found it still sticking in the letterbox. She must have been in a hurry, he thought, as he pulled it out; she usually read it over breakfast.

He worked in the garden doggedly for most of the afternoon, always hoping to hear the sound of Jo's car returning, but there was only the infrequent and distant sound of vehicles passing along their country road. When he was hungry, he stuck his spade in the soil and went into the kitchen to make a couple of sandwiches and drink another glass of diluted orange juice, leaving a trail of muddy footprints in the process. He had intended to go back out to the garden but there were things that Jo had asked him to do inside the house and which he had been ignoring on successive shore leaves. He did not like mending taps or banging nails into things but it might help him to get back into her good books if he started on the list.

His good intentions did not last long and he soon settled down with a packet of crisps and a beer to watch the news and then a games' show. He became so absorbed in the antics and judgements of the different contestants in the show, it was nearly seven o'clock before he looked up at the clock on the mantelpiece again.

He had no doubts now. She was avoiding him. Sometimes she ate out with friends but she always told him about it or left a note on the kitchen table. She also prepared a meal for him to heat up. Well, he would not rise to her provocation. He would act normally when she came in; ask if she had had a nice meal; and leave the remains of his uninspiring takeaway on the table to make her feel guilty about neglecting him.

On his way to the phone in the hall to ring the local Chinese, he noticed something different about the framed photographs and ornaments on the piano. They had been rearranged; it took him only a moment to realise that one of James's photographs had gone. In normal circumstances, he would have thought that there was a practical reason for that – the glass had broken or Jo had decided to replace it with another – but instinctively he knew that it was neither of these things.

He bounded upstairs and went straight to her wardrobe. He could not tell if anything was missing from there but her suitcase had gone from the cupboard above and her toothbrush was no longer hanging on the rack in the bathroom. He groaned in despair, unable to believe that she had been so angry and upset that she would go off and leave him without a word. He knew that she had been shaken when he had lost-it the previous evening; she had not said much but her stillness and the expression in her eyes had been enough to send him rushing out of the house.

She would be back. He knew that she would be back. Their shared memories and her sense of duty would not allow her to part from him for good. But he wanted more than that. He wanted her to love him; to return the love that she had given him so freely at one time.

3

Jocelyn was disorientated when she woke up the following morning, unable to work out why there were two, long, narrow windows to her left rather than a large one straight ahead; the light filtering through the curtains was giving shape to strange, bulky furniture – a large, carved mahogany wardrobe against the wall opposite, matching dressing table between the windows, a washstand beside the sink and a commode between the beds. For a heart-stopping moment she was alarmed and full of fear, and then it all came back to her. She had left Bill, and was now in a strange house on a remote island off the north coast of Scotland. She lay still, letting her thoughts roam and reshape, as she reflected on her tense experiences during the day before, the unusual people she had met and the situation she now found herself in. She knew that she was being vetted and it made her feel anxious.

A sunbeam briefly intensified the light in the room and she was immediately aware that the morning was well advanced; a glance at her alarm clock confirmed that. She threw back her bed clothes and padded across the carpet in her bare feet to open the bedroom door. She listened, but the only sound she could hear was the steady tick of the grandfather clock in the hall below. With no one about, she made a dash for the bathroom at the far end of the landing. The door was partly open and she pushed it wide, to be greeted by the nodding heads of well-known comedians suspended on the wall opposite. She bad them a 'good morning' and smiled when they seemed to respond with renewed vigour, as she closed the door behind her. The décor in the bathroom was bright and cheerful with an assortment of Phil's mobiles flying across the ceiling and a jumble of souvenirs from exotic places packed on shelves or left free-standing.

When she was showered and dressed, she took the stairs two at a time and hurried along the corridor to the kitchen. Bridget was the only one still there, sitting at the table with a book propped up against the marmalade jar. She closed her book slowly and interrupted Jocelyn's apologies for being late by saying languidly: "You can come down whenever you feel like it. Breakfast is a do-it-yourself affair."

"Has everyone else been down?"

Bridget shrugged, pushing herself up and ambling round to the Aga to put the kettle back on. She was packed into voluminous jeans with a loose smock on top, but the exotic effect was maintained with a beaded butterfly comb lodged in her hair. "Jason turns night into day and is seldom seen before dinner," she told her.

"And the others?"

"Hanna has taken a tray through to Rupert and Phil has gone down to the village."

Jocelyn relaxed. "I thought I was dreadfully late."

Bridget showed her where everything was kept by pulling out drawers and opening cupboards. "There's fruit juice in the fridge," she said, waving in that direction, "and eggs if you want something cooked."

"Just tea and toast," Jocelyn said, cutting a piece of bread from the cottage loaf lying on the bread board and dropping it into the toaster.

"I'll leave you to make your own tea," Bridget said,

undulating slowly back to her place at the table. She leaned forward on her forearms and watched as Jocelyn prepared her breakfast, ready to talk; but Jocelyn forestalled the inevitable, intimate questions by asking where Thorfinn was.

Bridget shrugged. "He could be out walking or sleeping late. You never can tell with Thorfinn." She smiled, lifting her arms to readjust her comb. "It is so good to have another woman in the house. Someone I can talk to. Hanna is not very communicative." She turned her head. "Oh, Hanna, there you are," she went on with no hint of embarrassment. "I was just saying to Jocelyn that it was nice to have another woman in the house."

"Yes, it is," Hanna said briefly, going towards the dishwasher and putting Rupert's tray down on the draining board. She looked distracted which could be because Rupert had eaten little of his breakfast.

"I've just made a fresh pot of tea," Jocelyn said. "Would you like a cup?"

"I had one with Rupert." That was all she said and the abruptness of the response made Jocelyn fear that she had heard Bridget's remark and might think that she was indulging in tittle-tattle. She blushed easily, which made her look and feel guilty, even when she was quite innocent, as now.

"How is Rupert this morning?" she asked.

"Much the same."

Jocelyn did not know how to reply to that. She glanced at Bridget but she was deep in thought and seemed unaware of what was going on around her.

"Did you have a comfortable night?" Hanna asked

pleasantly turning from the dishwasher with a smile.

"Oh, yes, very," Jocelyn babbled. "I slept so soundly, I didn't know where I was when I woke up."

"I hope the reality was not followed by regret."

"No, nothing like that."

"Well, once you've finished breakfast, I'll take you up and show you the vacant studio room."

"So I can stay."

"It's up to you."

"Yes, please."

"Phil will let you know his terms. They are very reasonable."

Jocelyn gulped down the remainder of her tea and started putting everything away, while Bridget complained to Hanna about Jason's nightly habit of knocking on their common wall.

Hanna did not immediately respond and Jocelyn could guess what she was thinking. Jason's sexual orientation made it unlikely that he was entreating sexual favours.

"Have you asked him why he is doing it?" Hanna asked reasonably.

"I have."

"What did he say?"

"He didn't say anything. He just turned away."

"Are you sure you didn't dream it?"

Bridget looked at Hanna balefully. "Nearly every night?"

"All right. I'll speak to him." She pushed herself away from the warmth of the Aga. "Ready Jocelyn?"

They wended their way up the circular staircase to the top landing. Unlike the floor below, this had only a rattan mat along its centre and the number of closed doors indicated that the rooms were smaller.

"Duncan and Phil did not use the rooms on this floor," Hanna told her. "There is a spiral staircase over there which leads to the attic. The previous owner floored it for his complicated train set and Phil has made that into his workshop." She opened a door in the corridor. "This will be your studio," she said, ushering Jocelyn in. "It is in quite a state, I'm afraid. Benjie did nothing with it."

The room was icy, the flowery wallpaper was peeling and there was only a scrap of carpet with a wide stained surround. There was a single bed in the middle of the room, covered with a sheet, and the brown veneered furniture was faded and scratched; the chest of drawers on the far wall seemed to be tipping forward and the wardrobe door was hanging open. Hanna went over and closed it but it just swung open again.

Jocelyn shivered.

"There's a radiator beside the bed," Hanna said quickly. "It's not on just now, but you can get up quite a fug when it is and Phil will fix the wardrobe door."

Jocelyn did not respond. Instead she crossed to the window which had a view of the back courtyard and a scrubby hill beyond. The excitement she had been feeling at staying was evaporating.

"I'm sure we can do something to make it a bit better," Hanna said, sensing her dismay.

Jocelyn started to cry. "I'm sorry, Hanna," she gulped, taking a handkerchief from her sleeve. "Take no notice. I get like this sometimes when I am under strain."

Hanna went over to stand beside her. "Quite frankly it

is awful," she admitted. "But you mustn't upset yourself."

Jocelyn blew her nose and gave a weak smile.

"We'll speak to Phil about it."

"No, you mustn't. It would be so rude."

"Don't worry. Phil has more than two pennies to rub together. He just needs things pointed out to him and he has them done."

And so it proved to be.

Jocelyn was making a rough sketch of a spread of deep purple crocuses in the walled garden, when he found her.

"My dear girl," he began, coming towards her across the wet grass with outstretched hands. "My dear girl," he repeated, his distress making him unable to find the right words. His jowls quivered with emotion.

"It's all right, Phil," Jocelyn assured him, getting to her feet and putting her sketch pad into her anorak pocket so that he could not see what she had drawn. She allowed her hands to be grasped. "I was just being silly."

But Phil would have none of it. He was mortified to think that she would judge his hospitality by the state of the room she was being offered. He assured her that everything would be done to make it just how she wanted it to be. Jocelyn smiled at the picture of misery he presented. His shoulders were slumped and the contours of his face drooped, accentuating the deep bags under his eyes. Impulsively, she went up on tiptoe and kissed him on the cheek. The transformation was immediate.

"That's better," he said, brightening up and giving her a fatherly pat on her back, before tucking her arm into his. "We don't want any tears in this house."

They started walking along the path that circumvented the garden. The hard soil in the herbaceous border was broken in places where frost had bitten into the rivulets of rain water that had lain on its surface during the winter, and the leftover clumps of withered plants were wispy and brittle.

"I shouldn't cry at my age."

"You were releasing a genuine emotion. No harm in that, but we must see that nothing makes you want to cry again." They had reached the vegetable garden where there were some vestiges of life. Winter cauliflowers and cabbages could be seen under home-made cloches and large wooden tea chests covered several patches of growing rhubarb. "We do not want to add to your sorrow."

"You have all been very kind to me."

"But I think it was loneliness that brought you to my door. Is that not so?"

"Partly."

Phil released her arm and lifted several cloches before selecting his choice of cabbage, its outer leaves yellow and withered. "Bereavement is hard to bear at any time but it is especially hard at your young age."

Jocelyn did not immediately respond and the silence palpitated between them. Eventually she whispered: "I cannot talk about it".

Phil assured her that he understood how she felt.

"I'm sorry I made a fuss."

"There now, say no more about it." They had reached the garden gate and he pushed it open, letting her pass in front of him before bolting it shut against the prevailing wind. "I'll get Tom Nicol to come in and sort the joists and then you and Hanna can make everything nice."

"Thorfinn has offered to help me paint it," Jocelyn said,

as they started to cross the courtyard to the back door. "I would like to do that. It would make me feel at home."

"Just as you wish. Meanwhile, we will spread a plastic sheet over the carpet in the spare room and you can make that your studio temporarily."

"I'll be very careful."

"Don't worry if you spill. Sometimes accidents happen."

"I use watercolour so it won't be too messy."

"Watercolour is the best medium for delicate flower paintings."

"You don't mind?"

Phil wriggled his bushy eyebrows quizzically.

"I mean about me liking to paint flowers best."

"Why would I mind?"

"Just something Rupert said last night."

"What did he say?"

"I can't remember exactly what he said but he implied that you didn't like representational art and particularly not flower painting."

"That's not so." Phil scraped his shoes on the scraper at the back door and Jocelyn followed suit. "I can see where he was coming from, but you don't like or dislike people because of their artistic preference."

"I'm not a very good artist," Jocelyn said charily.

Phil smiled. "You will not be judged, I assure you. The main thing is that you enjoy your work and get personal satisfaction."

"I do."

Once inside the house, Phil asked if she was going upstairs. The back stairs started there with an exit on each landing; a small corridor led through to the main hall.

"I haven't unpacked yet."

"You go and do that and I'll bring up the rest of your luggage."

Jocelyn turned, with one foot on the bottom step "Thank you Phil. Thank you for making me so welcome. I know I'm going to be happy here."

"That's what I want to hear. No more tears, now."

4

The old furniture in Jocelyn's studio was thrown out and the local joiner adapted take-home bedroom units and attached them to the walls; that way the floor boards did not need to be taken up and the joists repaired, which would have been a major undertaking. The room was still small and the two windows, cut into the deep stone wall, gave minimal light, but she was content. She had her own space within the house.

The sound of crunching gravel and the skid of wheels as a car swung round the side of the house and came to a stop, broke her concentration. She put down her paint brush and went over to the nearest window. If she stood to the side and looked down over the sill, she could see most of the back courtyard.

It was Thorfinn.

She watched him as he got out and opened the nearest of the three garage doors, leaving his engine running; by the time he had parked his car and closed the door down, Hanna had joined him, walking quickly across the courtyard with open arms. Thorfinn pulled her to him and kissed her several times, laughing with exuberance between each kiss. They linked their arms around each other and ambled across the flagstones towards the side door, beneath her window.

Before they disappeared from view, Thorfinn looked up.

It was too late for her to draw back so she opened the window wide and leaned over the sill, calling a greeting and welcoming him home.

"I'll be up to inspect our handiwork later," he responded with a wave, dropping his arm from Hanna's shoulder.

"Everything is finished," she replied, returning his wave.

Hanna was already inside the house. She had not glanced up or stopped to acknowledge Jocelyn's greeting. Jocelyn had got to know her better during the preceding weeks but there was a reticence on Hanna's part that kept them from becoming close friends. She was willing to help Jocelyn get settled, lending her sewing machine to make curtains and helping her work out a pattern to use the extra material on the plain bedspread, but she never allowed their conversations to become personal. Jocelyn knew as little now about her complex relationship with the three men in the house as she did on her first evening.

She went back to her painting. It was a work of imagination inspired by a shallow bowl of fruit, the apples and oranges tumbling over each other and toppling over the side of the dish. She had painted some tiny faces on their indentations or stems, the expressions she had given them depending on where they found themselves in the seemingly chaotic melee. It was quite different from the first paintings she had done in the walled garden. When Bridget had seen them, she had said that Jocelyn's style was too cramped and she should be freer with her brush strokes, but Jocelyn liked putting in neat and organised detail. She had expected Phil's reaction to be even more critical (her paintings were the antithesis of expressionism) but he had viewed them seriously and said that her detailed work would lend itself well to flights of fancy.

"Just for fun," he had suggested, "try giving your flowers and plants personalities, based on their shapes and toughness or fragility."

"I used to copy the flower fairies when I was a child," she had told him, with a nostalgic smile. "I really believed that there were fairies living in the cups of the flowers."

"A good start."

"It would be too difficult."

"Try it and see," he had advised, and had gone on to tell her how he had been a carpenter when he met Duncan and was encouraged to develop his talent for making odd ornaments. She had protested that she could do nothing like his quirky masterpieces but he would have none of it, saying that practice made perfect. This was her first attempt at humour, the pitted oranges and rosy apples suggesting expressions as they performed their tumbling antics.

There was a knock on her door; a rat-a-tat-tat, so she knew it was not Bridget. Bridget only gave one discreet tap.

"Hold on a sec," she called, moving farther into the room so that the door could be opened. "Come in now."

Thorfinn was full of his usual high spirits on arriving home for the weekend. His sun-streaked hair was on-end and his cheeks bright, after driving across from the airport with his roof down. She found him very attractive. He was full of charisma; his deeply-set grey eyes were nearly always a-twinkle and his wide mobile mouth turned up at the corners, reflecting his good nature.

He stood in the middle of the room, looking all

round and taking in every detail. "I think we'll go into the interior decorating business, partner," he said with a chuckle. This was, of course, an exaggeration. All they had done was strip the peeling wall paper and paint everything white, to reflect as much light as possible. "I love your curtains and the hideous carpet."

Jocelyn smiled, glancing down at the offending carpet. "It was chosen with care," she told him. "Any droplets of paint will just add to the overall splashes of colour."

He threw himself down on her bed, turning to prop up the pillows so that he had a comfortable head-rest. "We didn't manage to fill in all the cracks though," he commented, indicating the ceiling.

"They reappeared."

"They always do."

"Thorfinn, can I ask you something that has been worrying me?"

"Ask away."

"Phil advertised for "travelling artists" which sounds as if he was offering accommodation to people who were only visiting Trowsay for a short time."

"I don't think he knew what he wanted. It was Hanna who suggested that he take in boarders and he came up with the idea of artists."

"The thing is, we agreed that I should pay a monthly sum into his bank account. It is due again. Do you think I should assume that I can stay another month?"

"Ask him."

"I did ask him."

"What did he say?"

"He just looked puzzled and anxious, wondering if everything was all right. I assured him that everything was splendid." She picked up her brush and sucked the fine hairs into a point.

"So why are you worried?"

"Well, he didn't give me a straight answer. The conversation went off at a tangent, and then he said, out of the blue, that I didn't need to make another bank transfer. That left me wondering if it was his way of saying that my time had come to an end."

"He probably thought that you couldn't afford to stay and was waiving your monthly dot."

"I thought about that, but I hadn't said anything to make him think that I couldn't afford it."

"Relax! He likes having you here. We all do."

Jocelyn felt herself blushing and quickly dipped her brush into the water container.

"You are ravishing when you blush, Jocelyn."

She flicked the water-sodden brush at him but he ducked in time and through a pillow at her in response. She returned it with force and he caught it, laughing as he stuck it behind his head again.

"So what's been happening in the art world since I left?" he asked,

"Bridget says that she has nearly finished her stained glass window for Trowsay House but she won't let me see it."

"She won't let anyone see it. Bridget is a bit of a pain. We're hoping that she'll move on after the window is installed."

"How long has she been here?"

"Too long. And Jason? What has he been up to?"

"He is taking up conceptual art."

"You mean he is spending his days in bed."

"Well, it does seem to take a lot of thought."

Thorfinn laughed. "And you? I have resisted looking at your unfinished work."

"I have changed my style. From pernickety and boring to pernickety and humorous. At least, I hope it is humorous."

"As Phil suggested."

"It is absorbing and fun but not easy."

"Let me see."

She turned the easel and he gave a whistle of admiration but his gaze did not linger on it.

"And Rupert?" he asked. "How is he fairing?"

Jocelyn mixed some paint on her palette and tried the colour out on a scrap of paper, adding some more blue. "He is getting weaker. He still comes through in the evenings but he falls asleep, sometimes in the middle of a sentence." She saw her opportunity to probe. "Has Hanna not told you about him?"

"We don't mention the laird."

"The laird?"

"My name for Rupert."

Jocelyn looked quizzical.

"He tried to lord it over the island after he bought Trowsay House and turned it into a hotel. His superior manner dictated his nickname."

"He is rather over-bearing," Jocelyn agreed. "In fact, I find it strange that he and Phil are friends. They are so different."

Thorfinn gave a cynical laugh. "Duncan was a famous artist. He was someone to know and be seen knowing."

"And Phil?"

"Who could dislike Phil?"

Jocelyn nodded while concentrating on making the stem of an apple into a thin hooked nose between rosy cheeks. She put two tiny dots on either side and stepped back from her easel to assess the result, wrinkling her nose before adding two eyebrows, raised in surprise, on the indent circling the stem. She did not want these additions to be obvious, so that the viewer's first impression was of a straight forward still life, with the quirky additions only coming to light with further observation.

"Why don't you mention Rupert?" she asked, rotating her brush in the water and smoothing it into shape, before putting it upright in the container beside her.

Thorfinn made a face, reminding her of the house rule.

"I know I shouldn't be personal but I can't help being curious."

"Naturally, you're curious. I don't mention Rupert because I hate the bastard and wouldn't be able to hide my disappointment on hearing that he was no worse than he was a week ago." He swung his legs off the bed and pressed down on the mattress with his hands. "Up until three months ago, Hanna and I were living happily together in a twosome."

"My goodness!" Jocelyn exclaimed, turning to him in surprise. "Here on Trowsay?"

"No, down south. Hanna left Rupert nearly two years ago."

"So why did you come back? What happened?"

"Phil happened. He heard that Rupert was in a nursing home, dying of lung cancer, and had an ambulance bring him up here." Thorfinn got up and looked out of the window, his back to her. "He rang and told Hanna."

"She didn't need to come."

"You don't know my Hanna. Her conscience tormented her and it would have been cruel if I had not let her go. This life," he swept his arm around, "is our compromise."

Jocelyn said quietly, in an attempt to give him some comfort: "It won't be long now."

"That's what we thought at the start."

"He will soon need proper nursing and will go into hospital."

"I don't think so. Phil will organise something to keep him here."

"Have you spoken to him about it?"

He shrugged. "It's up to Hanna to decide."

Jocelyn thought that he should have some say in the matter but she did not voice her thoughts; instead she asked if the Selkie Bay farmhouse had belonged to Hanna's family.

Thorfinn looked at her in surprise and then chuckled, his gloomy mood passing. "Hardly. Have you seen the place?"

"I thought it might have been a holiday home."

"No, nothing like that. The house belonged to Alec Maconachie, a bachelor farmer who died a while back. A neighbour wanted the land but sold the house to us."

"You've been planning to return for some time then?"

"We were both home-sick. Hanna loved living here and Trowsay was my home for the greater part of my life. I did odd jobs at Trowsay House during my student days and latterly I existed on a pittance, so that I didn't have to leave."

Jocelyn stood back to assess her additions. "Did you and Hanna run away together?" she asked, voicing her curiosity.

He laughed and teased her for the romantic picture she had created, adding: "I was already working south when Hanna made the break."

"So living on a pittance lost its magic?"

"Touché." He watched Jocelyn tidying away her paints, before admitting: "I suppose you could say that I followed one love south and another one back."

Jocelyn smiled to herself. "It sounds as if your heart rules your head."

"That's how it should be, don't you think?"

She did not reply immediately, thinking of her own circumstance. "It is not always wise to allow emotion to dictate action."

"Not always, I agree, but…"

They could hear quick steps approaching the door and Hanna's voice calling: "Are you there, Thorfinn?"

"Coming."

Hanna pushed the door open against the easel "Sorry, Jocelyn," she apologised and, half into the room, spoke to Thorfinn: "Rupert has fallen in the shower room and Phil can't get him up."

"Is Jason not about?"

"There's no sign of him anywhere."

Thorfinn manipulated himself round the easel and she could hear him saying as they hurried along the landing: "It might bring on one of his rages if he sees me."

"But we can't just leave him there."

Their voices faded.

Jocelyn finished clearing away her paints and brushes and went through to the bathroom to tip out the water and wash the container, wondering all the time what was happening downstairs. Rupert lived in the drawing room on the ground floor where Phil's partner had had his studio. The downstairs shower room was across a corridor behind the kitchen but it was not large and she had wondered how Rupert manipulated his wheelchair in.

She finished tidying up and was ready for her walk. Unless the weather was appalling, she always walked at that time of the evening so she had a reason for going downstairs. Her anorak was in the porch but she slipped out of her sandals and pulled on lace-up boots. It was rough walking over the hill.

As she started down the last flight of stairs, she could hear Thorfinn and Hanna talking quietly in the hall. They looked up as she appeared.

"Is Rupert all right?" she asked, glancing over the banister.

"Phil managed him," Hanna said, only turning her head long enough to give that minimal response. Jocelyn felt snubbed and walked quickly to the porch door, the blood rising to her cheeks. It was the first time in the weeks that she had been there, that she had felt excluded.

"Enjoy your walk,"Thorfinn called and she raised her arm in response.

Phil's porch always had a magical effect on her, making her smile as she searched for surprises, but she only stopped long enough to lift her anorak from its personalised hook. Once outside, she breathed deeply, leaning against the heavy front door and chiding herself for being inquisitive. Phil had made her feel like a member of his adopted family but the relationship was an illusion. They rubbed along together but they were all very different.

She took the path through the shrubbery at the side of the house and into a grove of trees. The thickness of their trunks indicated that they had been planted in the distant past, no doubt in an attempt to give shelter to the shrubbery and greenhouses built there, but the irregular spaces between each one, suggested that a number had succumbed to the weather and salt air; those that had survived the winter storms were stunted, with ragged, twisted branches, bent by the wind. She walked on past the neglected greenhouses, with their unpainted struts and broken panes, and out into an open vista of heather and moor running right down to the Atlantic Ocean. There was a path of sorts but the heather had not been kept in check and it wandered at random, with rabbit holes here and there to entrap an unwary foot.

When she reached the folly near the cliff top, she sank down into the crown of coloured mosses on the headland. The folly was unusable. It was a stone-built construction with pillars and domed roof, but the sheep grazing on the hillside had sought shelter there and it was deep in excrement, the odour of the decaying matter dictating her choice of resting place. She spotted a man bending over a dormant ewe lying on the long grass near the top of a faraway cliff. He had a rope attached to the ewe's hind legs and was moving it round into position before hoisting the rope over his shoulder. He started dragging it up the slope towards a truck parked near the Atlanticscape drive. The other sheep watched them pass by, their mouths still and their eyes curious, but they soon lost interest and returned to their grazing. She wondered if the ewe had died of old age or if it had fallen over the cliff. Something to talk about at dinner.

Her gaze wandered at random along the jutting spits of land that enclosed secret rocky bays to the harbour and village in the distance, and back over the uninterrupted expanse of ocean, sparkling in the sunlight. The rhythmic splashing of the waves against the cliffs below had a hypnotic effect and she lay back, feeling, smelling and tasting the moist aquatic air. The soft spongy mosses made a comfortable bed and she was drifting between wakefulness and sleep, when flapping wings and shrieks from a pair of disputing terns made her sit up in alarm.

She had been thinking about Bill and wondering where it would all end. He would be lost without her but his dependence sapped her energy, and his renewed sexual desire brought tears of shame to her eyes. It was cruel to drop out of his life as she had done, but she needed time to come to terms with her past and if he knew where she was, he would not let her be.

Of course she would have to make contact eventually .... but not yet.

5

Bill put his rucksack down on the doorstep and took out his wallet to pay for the taxi. The front door was closed and there was no sign of Jo.

"See you," he said to the driver and watched him go down the short drive before trying the door. It was locked. He got down and unzipped his rucksack, rummaging in the inside pocket for his house keys. They were not there and he had to go round to the shed and get the spare set from the toolbox. As he walked back, he looked up at the unlit windows in the two-storey house. The place seemed desolate, and its emptiness was confirmed when he turned the key in the lock and pushed the door open against a heap of mail, lying thickly on the tiles inside.

She's not back, was his first thought as he walked through the carpet of paper, relieving some of his irritation by kicking the envelopes to the side with force; but when he opened the inner door, he was stopped dead in his tracks by the putrid smell that assailed his nostrils and gagged his throat. It was more than the mustiness of an unclean house. It was the smell of rotting flesh.

"Jo! Jo darling," he called out; his call was little more than a whisper, the words caught and swallowed in his restricted throat. He dropped his rucksack and ran up the stairs, his heart pounding. He feared that he would find her in bed, long dead, but it was only the air that was dead in that part of the house.

The smell got stronger as he careered downstairs,

following it round the stairwell to the kitchen at the back. He expected to find Jo's body crumpled on the floor, but all that was lying there was a bag of rotting rubbish containing unwashed tins, mouldy fruit, half-eaten takeaways and the left over meat that he had thrown out before leaving for the rigs. He had forgotten to take the bag outside to the bin. The sour smell coming from the bottle of milk and carton of cream, left lying on the table, added to the foul odour.

"Christ!" he exclaimed, unlocking the back door and lifting up the bag to take it outside. It promptly burst and spewed its contents over the vinyl tiles. The smell was even worse then and it still lingered long after he had brushed up the contents and got rid of them. He left the back door open and took a beer from the fridge, pulling the ring as he walked through to the sittingroom. The mess in there was just as he had left it two weeks before: grey ashes in the fire; a tray on the coffee table with the remains of an Indian takeaway, some on a plate and some still in greasy containers; empty beer cans beside the couch; shoes left lying where they had been kicked off; old newspapers strewn about; and the cushions indented at one end of the sofa where he had lain watching television. He had an eerie feeling of time having stood still.

There were two long messages from him on the ansaphone, giving Jo his news, saying how much he was missing her and sending his love. There was no message from her. He knelt down in the porch, picking up bundles of mail and discarding the catalogues and charity letters as he hunted for a card or a letter; there was nothing. He sat back on his heels in the sea of paper feeling bereft. Something must have happened to keep her from letting him know that she was delayed. She had said on her postcard that she was taking her mother on holiday, but she could not still be on holiday.

He disliked her mother who was always coming up with one story or another to get Jo to wait on her hand and foot; he doubted her invalidity. She had been at the wedding but he could not even remember what she looked like now and he had not been interested in Jo's visits; he had barely listening to her answers when he had enquired about her mother's health and their time together. All he knew was that she now lived in Dundee and had no telephone.

His lack of any concrete information counted against him when he rang the police to report her missing. The constable asked where Jo's mother lived. He could answer that, but the man wanted him to be more precise and he had to admit that he had not been able to reach her because she had no telephone and he did not know her address. The silence at the other end of the line spoke volumes.

"She has no reason for staying away," Bill said indignantly, forestalling the inevitable question.

"I'm sure the matter can be cleared up," the constable said smoothly. "No doubt the address you need is noted down somewhere. Have a look around for an address book or a letter."

Of course the constable was right. Jo must still be with her mother, otherwise he would have heard from her, and the address would be around somewhere. He could send a card, carefully worded, of course, because she must still be annoyed with him. They didn't always see eye to eye and he knew that she didn't like his untidiness; in fact, that could be the trouble, he convinced himself, as he tidied up his mess in the sittingroom and carried it through to the bin.

He phoned for a takeaway and, while he waited for its delivery, he drafted and redrafted a message until he got it right. "Everything spic and span but empty without you. All my love as always", was the version he hit upon. No accusations. No anger at her desertion. Just an informative, appreciative word or two.

The constable was right. The address would be in her desk or in the kitchen drawer where she kept the unpaid bills.

He was dead beat now but he would look for it in the morning.

6

The house was silent when Jocelyn came in from her walk. Was it the silence of death, she wondered as she went up to her room; but when she came downstairs for dinner, she heard the strains of Danny Boy coming from the radio in the kitchen, with Phil's baritone joining in from time to time. The trepidation she had been experiencing at meeting everyone in a house of mourning passed and made her bold enough to put her head round the door and add her voice to his, making a duet of "Danny Boy, oh, Danny Boy, I love you so."

Phil gave her a smiling welcome, beckoning her in. The table was already set for dinner, the variety and shape of the pictured placemats lending interest to the plain wooden table. Phil had a large and eclectic stack of mats in the dresser and he made a different selection each night. Sometimes he asked them to guess the place he had selected for them on the basis of their personality. He did not always get it right. Jocelyn remembered the hilarity when Bridget chose the place that he had earmarked for Rupert.

"Now that you are here, you can chop the cabbage for me," Phil said, moving a place setting back so that she could sit at the table and work. "I like it done like this." He cupped his hand round the loose-leaved vegetable and started to slice it thinly before relinquishing the job.

Jocelyn was pleased to help and told him so. She had offered to do her share at the outset, but Phil had said that he preferred to have the kitchen to himself, as he prepared the meal.

"I like to see you all relaxing with a drink after your labours," he told her, when she reiterated her willingness to help.

Jocelyn sliced in silence for a moment before saying: "Duncan's paintings are very colourful and unusual."

"Not to your taste though."

"I wouldn't say that. I am just uneducated in that style of painting."

"Why don't you choose one that you are drawn to and we can discuss it together."

"I'll do that." She lifted the chopped cabbage into the pan beside her and put the lid on. "How is Rupert?"

Phil took the pan from her and splashed in a minute amount of water before putting it on the hotplate. "It won't be long now."

"Can you manage him by yourself?"

"Not any longer. Did you hear about his fall?"

Jocelyn nodded.

"Hanna can't take much more. I have lined up nursing care but it will not do. She cannot give Thorfinn her full attention during his weekends home and it is getting her down."

"Thorfinn was telling me about it."

Phil turned to her in query. "What was he telling you?"

"Just the rather odd set-up."

"Does he blame me for bringing her back?"

"I don't think so," Jocelyn lied, with only the slightest hesitation.

"I'm sure he does." Phil finished making the gravy in the roasting pan and gave it a last stir before pouring it through a sieve into the sauce boat standing on the side of the Aga. "He swept Hanna off her feet, you know, but her loyalty was always divided. I never knew Thorfinn well when he lived here, but Rupert and Hanna were our closest friends and I always kept in touch with Hanna." He put the sauce boat on the table with its ladle and turned to lift the foil off the roast lamb which had been left to rest. "I had to tell her when I found out that Rupert was dying."

"You have nothing to blame yourself for. She chose to come back."

"I didn't think he would live for more than a few weeks then."

"Perhaps having Hanna in attendance gave him a reason to go on living."

Phil nodded slowly in response, lifting the carving knife and starting to sharpen it against the steel rod he held in his other hand.

"Everything is ready now," he said, the repetitive rhythm, back and forward against the steel, seeming to relax him. "Thanks for your help and for being a willing ear. I needed to unburden myself."

"We all need to sometimes."

Jocelyn found Thorfinn sitting in the parlour with a drink in his hand, conversing amicably with Bridget. He noted her surprise at seeing him there and said, with a wry smile: "Rupert is not coming through tonight so I'm able to partake of a civilized meal for once, instead of skulking upstairs with a tray."

"That's nice."

"You're much more stimulating company," Bridget flattered. "Rupert is not my sort of man. Too domineering and self-centred."

"Where's Jason?" Jocelyn asked.

"Gone."

"Gone where?"

"Off to join our recently departed Benjie."

"Without a word?"

"He rang Phil about an hour ago. A drink, Jocelyn?"

She shook her head, saying that dinner was ready.

Bridget levered herself up, readjusting her sari. She always changed into a sari in the evenings but she was not Asian; her colouring and accent were distinctly Irish. That evening, she was wearing a yellow silk one, with a flower woven into the intricate swirls of her chignon. Her nightly, exotic finery enveloped and embraced her full curves as she walked.

"Did you ever find out why Jason knocked on your wall at night?" Jocelyn asked her, as they wended their way towards the kitchen.

"I did not," Bridget replied forcefully. "He denied doing anything of the sort when Hanna asked him about it, but I assure you that he did."

"Perhaps he was literally banging his head against a brick wall in frustration at not being able to create the artistic image he could see in his mind's eye."

Bridget pooh-poohed that suggestion. "Jason was never going to be an artist," she scoffed. "Like Benjie, he was just looking for a place to stay."

Phil heard her and retorted: "It did not matter."

"But you wanted artists; serious artists like Jocelyn and me."

Thorfinn's eyes twinkled as he pulled out Bridget's chair. "Very serious," he said with mock solemnity.

"Especially Jocelyn's roly-poly fruit."

"I should have said committed."

Jocelyn smiled but did not say anything. She liked living and working at Atlanticscape, but she could not claim to be more than a competent amateur artist, exhilarated when a painting turned out well but with many disasters that had to be scrubbed out or torn up.

"Has anyone called Hanna?" Phil asked, lifting several slices of meat on to the top plate in front of him.

"She's upstairs changing."

"No, I'm here," Hanna replied, coming into the room and slipping into the seat beside Thorfinn. He put his arm around her shoulders and drew her to him momentarily.

"So, what have you all been doing today," Phil asked as he laid the roast back on the side of the Aga and took his place at the head of the table.

"Well, I've finished my window…."

"Can we come and see it now?" Thorfinn asked.

"You will see it when it is in place," Bridget said with a smile of self-satisfaction. She kept her door locked. Not even Patsy Gunn (who came in twice a week to clean) was allowed into her room. "You cannot experience the full effect of the colours and their juxtaposition unless there is light shining on and through the glass."

"I will curb my impatience with fortitude," Thorfinn said with mock gravity, but Bridget took his response literally and said that it would be well worth waiting for.

"I saw you going out," Jocelyn commented. She had been surprised to see Bridget cycling down the drive. Her shape did not seem to indicate that she would choose that mode of transport but she was obviously a competent cyclist because she had avoided the potholes expertly with barely a wiggle of the handlebars.

"I decided to cycle to the cave."

"Was the tide in when you got there?" Phil asked and Bridget turned her head slowly to regard him with astonishment.

"Do you mean that there would have been no water in the cave if the tide had not been in?"

"Only isolated pools."

"Then I was fortunate." She took the vegetable dish that was handed to her and helped herself liberally to cabbage. "The sun was only shining through the hole in the roof intermittently but I was entranced by the different textures of the rocks and how they changed colour and shape, as the water and seaweed lapped back and forward in the shifting light."

"There are particles of quartz, agate and flint in those rocks."

"I wouldn't know about that, but the experience has inspired me to make an impressionist stained glass plaque, to tide me over until I get another commission."

This statement was not greeted with enthusiasm.

"I did a sketch with coloured pencils when I got back."

"That sounds interesting," Phil said, before turning to Jocelyn and asking if she knew about their famous cave."

"I've seen a photo of it."

"The one taken from the sea?"

She nodded and told them about the book of photographs that she had bought on her journey up.

"Did it have accompanying prose?" Phil asked, passing the wine bottle down the table for everyone to help themselves.

"Well, there was a poetic caption, but it was just imaginary stuff. Something to do with trolls dancing."

Thorfinn chortled. "Shadow dancing by moonlight. It's a well documented fact."

"I think it is a myth rather than a fact, Thorfinn," Bridget corrected him, filling her glass.

"The documentation is a fact."

"It is certainly part of Trowsay folklore," Phil put in.

"And how Trowsay got its name."

"I must borrow the bike and visit this cave. Where is it exactly?"

"About a mile past the village along the coast road."

"It's pretty arduous cycling for the last half mile or so," Bridget warned. "Just a rough, stony track most of the way. I walked that bit."

Phil offered to take Jocelyn in the landrover. "I want to visit again to take photographs," he went on. "I started a sculpture of it many years ago but it didn't work out. I'm thinking of trying again."

Bridget leaned forward in her chair and regarded him speculatively. "Fancy us both having the same idea. The subject would certainly lend itself to having coloured glass in the rocks and we could collaborate like we did with "The Old Woman who lived in a Shoe".

"It is very different," Phil mumbled, his expression showing the wariness of a trapped animal, scenting danger. He quickly back-tracked, saying that it was just taking shape in his head and might come to nothing.

"Well, the offer stands."

There was a pregnant silence for a moment or two, before Jocelyn asked Hanna how they were getting on over at the farmhouse.

"It's coming along. They were putting the slates on the extension this afternoon and will be starting on the barn soon."

"Everyone is talking about it," Phil enthused, obviously glad to have been rescued from an awkward situation. "Alec would be amazed to see the changes you've made."

"Do you think he would have approved?"

"I'm sure he would."

"That reminds me," Thorfinn said, putting his knife and fork together and patting his stomach, well satisfied "Davey was saying that Alec's cousin in Canada has still not been found. Evidently the address given in the will no longer exists. The house was pulled down years ago and replaced with a block of flats."

"Didn't you know about that?" Phil asked in surprise.

"It was news to me. Did you know, Hanna?"

"Yes, I did."

"Obviously my antenna has got blunted through living south for so long."

"No one knows where she is," Phil told him, collecting the plates as they were passed down the table to him. "They've advertised extensively and even got lawyers in Canada involved but nothing doing."

"Of course she's bound to have married and changed her name."

"But that could be verified from the records without much trouble."

"Perhaps she married a foreigner and lives in another country," Hanna suggested, interrupting their dialogue.

"Or died in another country."

"Or died young."

"There's a thought."

"Did she inherit everything?" Jocelyn asked. .

"No. Most of Alec's money was destined to build the raised road across to the mainland."

"How did you get across before?"

"There was a tidal causeway."

"Guarded by Davey," Thorfinn reminisced. He leaned forward, with his elbows on the table, to address Jocelyn. "Davey used to sit on a boulder down on the shore in all weathers watching the comings and goings. He still sits there from time to time, but we had a bench made for him up top, so that he could still pass the time of day with whomever he chooses."

"But he finds it draughty there," Phil said, getting up and lifting the dishes on to the draining board, ready to be put in the dishwasher. "He still rails against Alec and his newfangled idea of building a road up above when there was a perfectly good road down below."

"Hardly the same thing," Thorfinn murmured.

"Weren't you dead against the construction of the bridge too, Thorfinn?"

He gave a wry smile. "I opposed it when I was living here, but I'm glad to have it there now."

"There hasn't been any adverse environmental consequence."

"Not yet, Hanna, but there will be. My reason for gratitude is purely selfish."

They watched while Phil put on his oven gloves and opened the top oven door, letting the tang of cooked rhubarb, mingling with the sweet smell of freshly risen sponge, escape.

"My favourite," Thorfinn said, giving a long, loud sigh of contentment. (He lived in a self-catering room during the week, counting the days until he was back at Phil's table)

"All our favourites," Jocelyn corrected him, taking the first plateful from Phil and passing it down the table. It was fortunate that they all liked rhubarb, she thought as she tucked in, because it was served up in one form or another, with different accompaniments, two or three time a week; but she had noticed that the strawberries were starting to turn in the large garden greenhouse and there were lots of raspberry canes there, white with flowers. Lettuces, cauliflowers and herbs were also being brought on under glass and, as the summer progressed, there would be every variety of northern fruit and green vegetable from the large walled garden. Phil worked there in the very early hours of the morning when everyone else was still a-bed.

"Would you like Jason's studio?" Phil asked, breaking into her thoughts. "It is bigger and has more light."

"I'm happy where I am," Jocelyn assured him, glancing towards Thorfinn and giving a smile of relief at having Phil confirm that she could stay on. Unfortunately their intimate exchange was intercepted by Hanna. Her expression did not change but her gaze lingered on Jocelyn reflectively.

She went red and blurted out an apology.

"No need to apologise," Phil said, misinterpreting her regret. "I didn't really think you would want to move. You have made your room so pleasant."

"Will you get someone else for Jason's studio?" Bridget asked, scraping her plate.

"I still have some enquiry letters but they are very out-of-date now." Phil got up and opened a drawer in the dresser, taking out a small bundle of envelopes. "Is there anyone there who might fit in?" he enquired, passing them round.

"I don't think so, Phil," Hanna said quietly. "We have already been through them and set them aside as unsuitable."

As each letter reached her, Jocelyn skipped through the contents. Two of the envelopes were brightly coloured and one still had a faint perfume of rose, no doubt in an attempt to woo the unknown Phil. One of the applicants took a whole page to write one sentence in a sloping scrawl and another, the only typewritten one, ran to four pages of single spacing. Hanna was right. None was suitable but she did not think it her place to say so. She wondered what she would have written and how her application would have been received. She would have been more literate than most, but her neat hand-writing would have marked her down as inhibited.

"I'll ring tomorrow and put another advertisement in," Phil said.

"A repeat of the last one?" Bridget asked in dismay.

"Why not?"

She gestured towards the pile of letters saying: "Don't you think that it encouraged unsuitable applicants?"

"I found it an intriguing advertisement," Jocelyn said quickly, to counteract Bridget's criticism. "It gave me all sorts of romantic notions about travelling artists plying their trade as they wandered through the countryside."

"And the reality was much more humdrum."

"Far from it, Phil; it is all wonderful. However when the die was cast and I was nearly here, I did wonder if I would find that your 'comfortable home' was an exaggeration and it was a hostel for down and outs."

Thorfinn laughed. "I can just picture you in a room full of bunk beds and grey blankets, Jocelyn. Not to mention the resident fleas."

"Perhaps we should rethink the wording," Hanna suggested. "The design does not need to be changed but...." She stopped mid-sentence and listened. "Was that Rupert's bell?"

"I didn't hear anything," Phil said.

"He shouldn't be awake yet," Hanna exclaimed in distress, pushing back her chair.

"I'll go."

"No, let me, Phil."

Thorfinn touched her hand as she got up, communicating his silent support, and watched until she was out of sight. He then said bitterly: "That bell will haunt me. I even hear it in my dreams when I'm away."

"Did you hear it this time?" Phil asked him. "Did anyone hear it?"

No one had.

"I think Hanna imagined it," he said, bundling the letters together. He got up and put them back in the dresser. "She is haunted by the fear of not hearing it when he needs her."

The words were barely out of his mouth before they heard Hanna's footsteps running along the corridor. She stopped in the doorway, her eyes wide and her breath coming in short gasps.

"What is it, Hanna?" Thorfinn asked, striding across and taking her in his arms.

"He's dead," she whispered, her legs starting to give way. "He was just lying there as I had left him."

"My poor darling. Shush now."

"Take Hanna to the parlour, Thorfinn," Phil said, sliding past them. "I'll see to everything."

There was a shocked silence after they left. Jocelyn and Bridget looked at each other but neither spoke. Bridget got up and started collecting the pudding plates together but Jocelyn sat on, wishing that she could spirit herself away.

"It's probably best if we make ourselves scarce," Bridget said, starting to load the dishwasher.

Jocelyn agreed.

"But we should tidy up in here first. If you sweep the floor, I'll do the sink and wash down the Aga."

Jocelyn agreed but she did not get up. Her legs felt weak; thoughts that she had successfully shut away, deep in her sub-conscious, were beginning to swirl to the surface.

"Come on, Jocelyn, snap out of it."

"Sorry. Let me help."

"Take everything off the table first."

Jocelyn did not speak but she began to collect the mats together.

"Phil will probably want to bring visitors in here for coffee or something and the least we can do is leave the place clean and tidy."

"I'm sorry, Bridget; it was all a bit of a shock."

"It was hardly a shock. It's been on the cards for weeks."

Bridget's matter-of-fact response to Rupert's death restored Jocelyn's equilibrium. Her fear of being involved in the formalities of death was unreal. She had hardly known Rupert and she lacked the closeness that would bind the family and their visiting neighbours together, during the days ahead.

"I suppose Phil will need our rooms for the relatives," Bridget said gloomily, filling a basin of water and lifting it out of the sink.

"I hadn't thought of that." The possibility cheered Jocelyn up. She would not need to find an excuse to leave until it was all over.

"I wonder what family he had."

"Two sons and a daughter," Jocelyn told her, taking the brush and dustpan out of the far cupboard and starting to sweep.

"Did Hanna tell you that?"

"No, Rupert."

"I suppose it was with a first wife." Bridget laid the basin on the side of the Aga and lifted the lid back. "But they've never been in touch while I've been here."

"I got the impression that there had been a rift but they would probably want to come to their father's funeral."

Bridget slowly washed the metal plate, droplets of sudsy water sizzling and scooting around on its hot surface. "I don't want to go back to my parents in Ireland, however briefly," she confided, ringing out the cloth and lowering the lid.

"It would be a long way to go."

"It's not just that. The atmosphere is unpleasant there. They didn't want me to marry Rajit and were delighted to be proved right when we parted."

"I didn't know you'd been married. Did you live in India?"

"If only!" Bridget exclaimed bitterly, wiping round.

"I'm afraid Rajit was more anglicised than I was."

"And yet you wear a sari."

"Much to his disapproval."

"It suits you."

"I know."

Jocelyn hid a smile as she swept underneath the table. Bridget had no false modesty which was unusual but refreshing. "Did he appreciate your artistic talent," she asked, resting momentarily on her brush.

"Rajit wanted me to be a full-time wife and mother but I wasn't suited to that role. I specialised in stained glass and I wanted to do that, not stand at the kitchen sink or wash stinking nappies."

Bridget's voice was scornful and Jocelyn could not help feeling sorry for the absent Rajit. He had obviously got more than he had bargained for in marrying Bridget.

"What about you?" Bridget asked, crossing to the sink to empty the basin and rinse the cloth. "Where would you go?"

"I haven't thought about it," Jocelyn lied, not wanting Bridget tagging along if she went off to explore the north of Scotland.

"You will need to think about it." Bridget advised, wiping round the sink and folding the cloth over. "Would you go home? You have never said why you came to Trowsay."

"I just wanted to get away for a bit and concentrate on painting." Her response seemed to satisfy Bridget because she did not press her for any more information. Her self-obsession did not make her over curious about others.

Phil was in the hall speaking on the telephone when they left the kitchen. He beckoned to them.

"Don't go up," he begged, replacing the receiver. "Go into the parlour and keep Hanna company."

"Isn't Thorfinn there?" Bridget asked.

"It's best if he disappears for a bit. Tell him that Miss Silver is on her way."

"Miss Silver?"

"The minister. She is very orthodox in her views."

Thorfinn was standing with Hanna beside the fire when they joined them and he was not pleased to receive Phil's message, pointing out that Miss Silver would have to get used to them being together.

"It will be different later," Hanna said quietly, moving out of his arms and gently pushing him towards the door.

"You mean you'll no longer be committing adultery," Thorfinn rejoined bitterly. "You are no longer doing so now. She has nothing to get worked up about."

"Don't be difficult, Thorfinn."

"All right, all right, you're the boss."

After he had gone, Jocelyn took Hanna's hands and squeezed them, murmuring her regret and conveying her support. The normal words of condolence did not seem appropriate in Hanna's situation.

Bridget was more demonstrative, pulling Hanna to her ample bosom and saying: "You can only feel relief, Hanna, dear. You did more than your duty in looking after him these last months."

Hanna extricated herself and turned away, putting a hand on the mantelpiece and looking down into the fire. "I do not feel relief, Bridget. I think of the pitiable state he was in at the end, and the months he had fighting his illness alone while I was with Thorfinn."

"But you didn't know."

Hanna did not reply and there was an awkward silence for a moment or two. "I don't want to involve you in my grief," she said eventually, turning from the fire. "You only knew Rupert when he was ill and crotchety, but I remember him as he was when we met and the happy years we had together."

They heard the door bell ring, followed by voices in the hall.

Phil ushered in an elderly woman, small and spare with wiry grey hair.

"Thank you for coming, Chloe" Hanna said quietly, crossing to meet her.

"My dear, of course I would come." She took both Hanna's hands and held them tightly. "I'm sorry that I stayed away so long."

"Rupert became difficult and argumentative towards the end."

"But I should have borne it." Miss Silver acknowledged Jocelyn and Bridget's presence before turning back to Hanna. "He is with God now, my dear, and that is a blessing. We will go and pray together."

After they left, Phil put more coal on the fire, the noise of his shovelling and the flaring of the new coals as they hit the bright embers had a mesmerising effect. There was only one lamp lit and the room was full of shadows.

"Sherry?" Phil offered, going across to the drinks' tray on the side table. "I think Miss Silver would accept us drinking a sherry. She might even accept one herself when she comes back."

They sipped their drinks, standing beside the fire. Jocelyn's eyes were drawn to one of the paintings. It had not caught her attention before; she had dismissed it, like all the others, as a type of abstract expressionism that she could not understand and never would. But now, in the shadowy room, she could see the overlapping colours separating and forming different shapes, advancing and retreating, in the flickering light from the fire.

"It was very sudden at the end," Bridget said, breaking into her thoughts.

"It might seem so, but he had had a bad fall earlier," Phil reminded her, gesturing towards the sofa and sitting down in the armchair opposite them. "That would have taken its toll on his emaciated body and his will to go on living."

Bridget agreed and went on to discuss a cousin of hers who turned his face to the wall and willed himself to die when he was left alone in the world.

Jocelyn took no part in the conversation.

"Are you all right, Jocelyn?" Phil asked. "You've gone very pale."

"I'm sorry. It's nothing, really." She smiled weakly. Phil was still looking at her with concern and she wanted to reassure him. "I was thinking that the relatives will be coming up for the funeral and you will need our rooms."

"If that's all that's worrying you, I can put your mind at rest," Phil said with a smile. "Rupert wants to be cremated, so the service will take place at the crematorium in Inverness."

"But won't some of his family want to come up here to finalise details and thank everyone for looking after him, that sort of thing."

"I won't invite them. Hanna must go down to the funeral service but it will be very awkward for her."

"I suppose they blame her for breaking up the marriage," Bridget said.

"It's not just that," Phil murmured, sipping his drink and looking into the fire thoughtfully. "They ostracised her. I suppose it is understandable in the circumstances but not pleasant. Rupert's children are Hanna's cousins."

"That doesn't seem possible."

"Rupert's first wife was Hanna's aunt – her mother's sister."

"Is that allowed?"

"It is certainly unusual," Phil admitted. "Hanna is half-Norwegian and was brought up in Norway. She didn't meet that family until she was in her late teens."

"You mean Rupert seduced his young niece!"

"Nothing of the kind," Phil flashed back, his bushy eyebrows working overtime."

Bridget said she was sorry but she lifted her chin and looked anything but sorry.

Jocelyn intervened: "You are assuming that Hanna was an unwilling recipient of his affections, Bridget, and that is obviously not true."

"But it is not right for an uncle to behave like that."

"She was not a blood relation."

Phil agreed, getting up and putting his glass down on the mantelshelf. He mumbled something about going to make more phone calls and headed for the door.

"I don't think I should have made any comment," Bridget admitted, when he had gone.

"No, you shouldn't have," Jocelyn said forcefully. "Rupert was Phil's friend."

"But you must admit, Jocelyn, that he took advantage of a young girl."

"I don't know anything of the sort, Bridget. Neither of us does."

"You sound upset, Jocelyn."

"I am upset. I don't want to talk about this."

Bridget wriggled forward on the sofa and pushed herself up with the help of the armrest, her glass balanced in the other hand. She knocked back the remains of her sherry saying: "I think it would be wise for me to seek my room before Phil comes back."

Jocelyn did not demur.

She stayed on in the parlour, keeping the fire going, but Hanna did not reappear. The door bell went several times and she could hear the familiar voices of the doctor, who had called regularly during Rupert's illness, and Tom Nicol. He was the undertaker, as well as the local joiner, and when Phil brought him into the parlour for a whisky, she made her excuses and went up to bed.

7

Bill sat in a bar near the railway station in Dundee. He had tracked Jo to an address there and had left home a day early so that he could stop off and make peace with her before going back offshore. He was quite confident that he would be able to gently smooth over any ripple of resentment and get back into her good books, so that next time he came back, she would be there to welcome him.

He just needed a bit of liquid courage first.

He was a pub man and what with this and that, a drink bought here and a dart thrown there, it was getting on for nine o'clock before he was on his way. By that time he had worked himself up into a state of indignation at being left without a word of explanation.

The taxi dropped him off outside a tenement building not far from the centre of town and he rechecked the address from the slip of paper he had in his wallet. He hadn't realised that her mother lived in such a seedy place. The building was black with decades of chimney smoke and traffic fumes, the windows were small and the vehicles outside moved in a steady flow, until stopped by the lights. There was some explicitly sexual graffiti on the wall of the building that someone had tried, unsuccessfully, to wash off.

However, inside it was quite different. The traffic noises were muffled by the thick walls and the stone stairs leading up to the different floors were clean with the walls painted in fuchsia and pale pink. There were four flats on each floor; he checked the numbers as he reached each landing, stopping at a panelled and varnished door, two flights up. There was both a knocker and a bell. He let his rucksack fall to his feet and tapped the knocker. When there was no reply, he pressed the bell firmly, listening keenly for any sound inside. He was beginning to think that there was no one there, and that Jo and her mother were still away on holiday, when the doorbell was answered by a tall, good-looking man.

Bill gaped.

"Yes?" was the enquiry.

Bill's shock quickly changed to belligerence. He was at the state of intoxication where he could believe that Jo had been lying to him all along and had a secret lover. In fact it could explain quite a lot.

"I've come to see Jo."

"I'm afraid you've got the wrong flat."

"This is Lower Commercial Road?"

"Yes."

"And this is 11?"

"Yes."

"Come off it then."

"I'm sorry." The man drew in his chin and pulled back his shoulders, his tone of voice making the words a reprimand, not an apology.

"You know fine who Jo is."

The man started to close the door but Bill put his foot in it.

"Go and bother someone else," he said, kicking Bill's foot away.

"I just want to speak to her."

A voice from within the flat called: "Who is it,

Gordon?" And a small, sharp-faced woman appeared.

"What do you want?" she asked, giving Bill the once over.

Bill was flummoxed. He looked at the number again. He had the right flat.

"Sorry," he said sheepishly. "I thought someone else lived here."

"Obviously."

"Have you lived here long?"

"What's that got to do with you?" the woman replied.

"I was looking for Mrs. Simpson's place."

"An elderly wife?"

"Yes."

"She moved out more than a year ago."

"Do you know where she went?"

"I've no idea. I only know the name because of the leaflets that come through the door: pensioner club outings and such like. In fact a card arrived a week or two back for someone living with her." She turned to her hall table and picked up Bill's card with its grovelling message. He did not claim it as his, or protest when the door was closed on him.

He felt deflated. There had only been the one personal letter in Jo's desk and it was undated, with a limited address and an illegible signature. He had spent some time at the library looking up telephone directories and using different interpretations of the scrawled signature, but he could not find any details of the person who had written it. It was only when one of Jo's friends telephoned that he was able to start tracing her. Now he was back to square one.

He trudged down the stairs and out into the cold

of the night. He could smell the exhaust fumes from the traffic and see the film of dust that polluted the air between the high buildings. What a place to spend one's life, he thought, as he swung his rucksack on to his back. He could not picture Jo living there.

He hailed a taxi and returned to the familiarity of the pub he had left, rejoining the darts' players and settling down to enjoy the rest of the evening. There was a certain relief in not having to face Jo and give an account of himself; she would be home next time and the place would be clean and tidy for her return. He had arranged for contract cleaners to give the place a good going over. She was always finicky about that sort of thing.

8

Thorfinn and Hanna went off on a walking holiday a few days after the funeral, and Jocelyn lost her urge to paint. The two events were loosely connected. For Jocelyn, death and the ritual of death had brought back painful memories and sapped her energy: some days she was lethargic, wanting to stay in the cocoon that Atlanticscape had spun round her, and some days she was restless, knowing that her stay there was only an interlude in her life.

The house was quiet. It had always been quiet but before it had been a calming quietness, allowing her to concentrate on her work without distraction; now it felt empty. Bridget was in an uncommunicative mood and Phil was up in his eyrie.

She buzzed him to ask if he would like a cup of coffee.

"If you're making it," he responded, but she could tell by his initial hesitation before speaking that he was immersed in creation.

She found him in the preparatory stage of carving a sculpture of the cave. He had moulded the rock stacks in clay, adding additional twists and protuberances to make them more like the trows or trolls pictured in Norse mythology, and he was trying to make their shadows dance against a card background with a revolving Christmas lantern. The glass inside the lantern circled slowly round giving flickering light and he was adding panels of card, taking them out, cutting and putting them back in, trying to get the effect he wanted.

"I'm nearly there," he said, taking the filled mug carefully by the rim and laying it down beside him. "Once I know that it will work, I can start on the wood."

She watched him for a bit, sipping her coffee, but he was absorbed in his work and had shut her out of his thoughts. She wandered over to the window where there was a large, round armchair that still had the faint smell of dog. It had been the day bed for Phil's ancient St. Bernard and nothing had been done to it since he died a few months back. She leaned against the shutter, cupping the comforting warm mug in her hands, looking down over the valley with its scattering of weary shrubs to the heavy sea in the distance. There was little colour or shape to the scene. It was a grey day; not even a bank of heavy cloud relieved the gloomy blankness of the sky. She fingered the wood round the small panes of glass in the window; the paintwork had been stripped by the sun and there was only the occasional fleck of white, sticking to the grained hardwood.

"If you're at a loose end, Jocelyn," Phil said, breaking into her desultory thoughts, "would you take a run over to Selkie and see how the men are getting on? We can give Hanna a progress report when she rings tonight."

Jocelyn agreed enthusiastically, her spirits rising now that she had Phil's attention and a purpose to her day. "And can I do anything for you in the garden?"

"No, it's all o.k. at the moment but there are one or two things we need from the shop." He drank down his cooling coffee in one go and laid the empty mug on the offered tray. "The list is in the purse."

She skipped down the attic stairs and collected her things together, shrugging into her anorak and picking up the purse from the kitchen drawer, before crossing the courtyard to the garages in the old stable block. Her car was sandwiched between Phil's landrover and the sit-on lawnmower, leaving only a small gap for her to open the door and squeeze into the front seat. She made herself comfortable and turned the key to start the engine; the battery was flat. There was just a whirr of the starter dynamo; not even a delicate cough that could be caught and nursed. Her light mood evaporated. It was going to be one of those days, she thought as she got out, kicking the back wheel in frustration on her way round to the boot for the jump leads. It was then that she discovered the reason for her flat battery: she had left the boot partly open on her return from visiting the bird sanctuary the day before. She got the jump leads out and attached them between her battery and Phil's, before climbing up into his landrover to start the process; it only needed a pump or two of his accelerator to bring life back to her dormant battery. She felt a bit guilty about not asking Phil first before making free of his car's energy but she did not want to disturb him again.

The job done, she eased her car forward, bumping down into the narrow drain outside the garage door and up on to the flagged courtyard. The courtyard had been surfaced to accommodate the hoofs of horses, not the weight of motor vehicles, and most of the grey flagstones were broken or flaking, dipping in places where the rain had penetrated and softened the soil underneath. She rounded the house and started to wend her way down the long drive, opening her window and breathing in the cool fresh air, with its briny whiff of wet accumulated seaweed drifting up from the shore.

She decided to do the shopping first.

The door bell tinkled as she went in. There was no one serving in the shop but it was clear where Cissie was and what she was doing because Jocelyn could smell onions frying somewhere in the back. She looked round while she waited. Trowsay's shop cum post office sold most things. In fact anything that would be needed in a hurry or would do the job in an emergency. There were even things that she did not think anyone would need nowadays. She could see a mesh-sided cupboard hanging from the ceiling at the far end of the shop and recognised it as the sort of thing that her granny had hung outside the back door in a shadowy spot to keep food fresh and safe from flying insects.

"Well, now, what can I do for you today, Mrs. Fenwick?" Cissie asked, parting the divisional curtain and wiping her hands on a cloth as she came forward, all smiles. She was a short, square woman in her early sixties, with rosy cheeks and a mop of tightly-permed hair, dyed light beige.

Jocelyn handed over the list and Cissie began to collect the groceries together, giving herself time to ask after the members of the unorthodox household up at Atlanticscape and tut over Jason's hasty departure. "I doubt if he'll be missed," she went on. "According to Patsy Gunn he was not going to set the art world alight and I could get nothing out of him when he came in here to buy his chocolate."

She bent over to scan the boxes of detergent on a bottom shelf, tottering and steadying herself as she straightened and refilled her lungs. "Tell Phil that there is an offer on this one and it is just as good," she said, dropping it into the basket at her feet. She did not wait for Jocelyn to reply, as this interruption to her flow of talk was only incidental. "We were all right glad to know that Phil had a respectable woman to turn to now," she flattered, with an ingratiating smile. "Mind you, I won't speak ill of the dead…" she pulled her nostrils together with an audible sniff "….or the living." Jocelyn knew that her antagonism towards the Treathams, dated back to the time when they had had the Trowsay House hotel and had bought their groceries at the supermarket over on the mainland. She did not add fuel to the fire of resentment by commenting.

"What has Phil written there?" Cissie asked, holding the shopping list at arm's length in an effort to make out what he had inserted right at the bottom, but by the time Jocelyn had reached her at the far end of the shop, it had been deciphered.

"Let me help you with that," Jocelyn offered and took some items from Cissie's laden arms, carrying them back to the till.

"Now then, what are you going to be up to today?" Cissie asked, turning to pick a bottle of sherry from the display of drinks behind her and starting to pack all the grocery items into an empty soup box.

"I'm on my way to the Selkie Bay farmhouse to see how the renovation work is progressing."

"It's progressing fine. They've got nearly all the cobbles and concrete up in the barn and will be laying down the damp proofing next," Cissie told her, adding, with a sly sideways glance: "They'll get on with it quicker now that she has the money to pay them regularly."

Jocelyn raised her eyebrows and Cissie was pleased to

be able to put her in the picture. "She's been managing on the money that Thorfinn made down south. She could not expect her husband to contribute to their nest building."

"Hanna was very good to Rupert."

"Ah, well, that's as may be but ......

Jocelyn listened as Cissie relayed the story of Thorfinn's involvement in the Treatham's separation and Hanna's subsequent return to Rupert. "I believe," Cissie went on, with a self-righteous lift to her chin, "that Mrs. Treatham saw where her duty lay at the end of the day, although there are some who say that her return was not through compassion for her husband in his terminal illness, but to ensure that he did not divorce her and leave his money elsewhere."

"That is shocking!"

"Aye it is and I tell them so."

Jocelyn really was shocked at the turn the conversation had taken and quickly changed the subject by asking for six bottles of wine to take back as a contribution to the household budget. The choice of wine was limited but she was fairly confident that the ones she chose would be acceptable.

"Are you going to take the main road or the coast road to Selkie?" Cissie asked,

"I didn't know I could get all the way along the coast. Phil and I visited the cave a few days ago but the road looked as if it was petering out."

"It goes as far as the Trowsay House cottages but you would have to walk the last bit round the bay to Selkie, and the track is in a poor state. You'd be best to go the long way round."

"Yes, I think I'll stick to the main road."

"Well, if you're going that way, you could drop this in at Shaws."

She lifted a box of groceries from behind the counter. "I've made a cake for him and tucked in a bit of ham."

"Where is Shaws?"

"It's the second turning on the left past the hotel. He'll be out on the farm but just leave the box on the kitchen table."

"He won't mind me going in?"

"Why would he mind?" Cissie leaned forward and lowered her voice. "Poor man, he was only married six months when his wife … she was our district nurse, you know … was killed in a head-on crash while out doing her rounds. Not here, mind, over there on the mainland."

"That's very sad."

"There's talk of him going back to Canada. His uncle willed him Shaws and that brought him over here in the first place but now there's nothing to keep him."

Jocelyn struggled to lift one of the boxes with her handbag dangling from her wrist.

"Ted!" Cissie called and a tall, thin man appeared from the back. "Mrs. Fenwick needs help with her groceries."

Ted came round the counter and smiled down at her. "How is the painting going?" he asked. They had met down at the pier shortly after her arrival. She had made a sketch of his lobster pots, set against the veined grey stone of the slipway. He had thought it was "right good" but she had not liked it.

"I'm having a day off," she told him, as he lifted a box and preceded her to the door. "Several days off, in fact."

"Bye now," Cissie called. "Tell Phil that I was asking

after him."

"I will. Thanks for your help."

"My pleasure."

Ted held the door open, the box resting on his hip bone. "Recharging your batteries, are you?" he asked, as he followed her out of the shop.

She stopped dead and he nearly walked into her back.

"I meant to ask if you sold car batteries."

"I don't have any in stock but I can get you one, if you need it," he said as she stood aside to let him pass. "Is yours giving trouble?"

She told him about finding it flat.

"You could recharge it overnight," he suggested, opening her boot and sliding the box in. "Phil will have a charger."

"But it should have been well charged with my journey up here."

"True enough." He left the boot open for the other two boxes and asked her how old it was.

"It came with the car."

Ted looked at the number plate. "Aye, it will be needing replaced," he said. "I'll have one here for you by tomorrow."

Before she left the car park, Jocelyn checked her map. She could see that the track round the coast went for quite a long way, stopping above a dwelling house on the near side of Selkie Bay. There was a path from there to the farmhouse and it would have been far more enjoyable to go that way, rather than following the main road down the length of the island and back up the other side of the loch. She wished that she had not agreed to deliver the groceries for Cissie but she had no choice now.

The Shaws' farmhouse was a two-storey structure of modest proportions built on a rise overlooking the loch. The track up led into a cobbled courtyard, which showed evidence of dairy cattle passing through earlier in the day. The back door was open but there was no sign of the farmer. Jocelyn knocked and called out but there was no reply, so she did as she had been bidden and took the box into the kitchen. She laid it on the table and looked round with curiosity. It was a bright cheery room, painted a pale daffodil yellow, the colour picked up and developed in the patterned tiles and the deep ceiling frieze. There were modern units and high tech equipment under the veined, pale marble worktops, a green fronted Raeburn, which gave warmth to the room, and a stained oak dresser displaying odd bits of patterned Wedgwood, in muted shades of blue and pale mauve. It was scrupulously clean and tidy. On the windowsill, there were containers of orchids and she was absorbed in admiring their different shapes and colours, wondering how she would paint them, when a voice spoke from behind her.

"You're a honey for bringing that over."

She got such a fright, she nearly fainted.

The man strode over and cupped his hands strongly round her upper arms until she regained her balance.

"Are you all right?" he asked, his voice troubled. She would have taken his accent for American if she had not been told that he was Canadian.

"I'm sorry. I didn't realise you were here or I wouldn't have trespassed."

He laughed, his hazel eyes sparkling with amusement. "You didn't trespass. You were doing me a favour by bringing my shopping over." He released his grip but stayed where he was, looking down at her quizzically. She was intensely aware of his closeness and it was having an effect on her legs and her breath that was quite different from that which she had experienced a moment before. He was a big man with a carroty top and a ruddy face, sprinkled with freckles. He wore a checked shirt, the arms rolled up to show strong, muscular arms and a fuzz of downy hair.

"You really are a honey," he said softly and she blushed. "Yum, yum."

"I must get on," she said, moving away.

"What's the hurry?" he questioned lazily, going across to the door and pulling his boots off. "I was just about to heat a bowl of soup. Sit down and take the weight off your feet." He pulled out a kitchen chair in invitation and turned towards the stove.

"It seems an imposition."

"No imposition. I could do with the company."

He put her at her ease as he stirred the soup by talking about Atlanticscape and the people who had come and gone over the past year. She had felt secluded and anonymous up there in the hills but it was clear that everyone knew who she was and how she fitted in.

"My wife was a close friend of Hanna," he explained as he poured the soup into bowls. "Since the accident.... you will have heard that Ursula was killed in a road accident...." Hanna nodded, expecting him to go on, but he said no more. He rummaged in the box of groceries and pulled out a packet of rolls and a slab of butter. "I see that Cissie has decided to feed me up," he went on. "Here's some home-baked ham and one of her cakes. Will we tuck into that?" He looked up for her agreement and she could see by the moisture in his eyes that reverting to the mundane was a device he used to keep his emotions in check.

They ate in silence for a bit.

"I still find it difficult to believe," he said, putting his spoon down. "Ursula was not the sort of person who got killed. She was always in charge of the situation."

Jocelyn could only listen as he relived their life together. She had not known his wife and so could not give comfort by adding to his memories but when he had finished, she told him about her sorrow. They drew comfort and intimacy from their related memories and as they sat over the remnants of their meal, the conversation drifted on to other topics. She found that he had not been a farmer in Canada, but a mountie. Jocelyn could imagine him up on a horse in the dress uniform of the Canadian Mounted Police. She smiled at the romantic picture this evoked and he smiled back. He knew what she had been thinking and this time it did not embarrass her. It was just a sign of the easy companionship that they had established.

"I hear you are selling up and going back," she said

"Am I?"

"Cissie was telling me."

He chortled. "I am going to Canada for ten days at the end of this week but it's just to keep up with the folks over there." He started to collect the dishes together. "Farming is in a bad way at the moment but it'll pick up. And you?"

"I am only passing through. Phil is very kind but I can't stay there for ever."

He opened the dishwasher and she handed the plates down. "Now that we have met, I would be sorry to see you go." He straightened and took her hand. "Come again soon."

He walked her to her car and leaned along her roof as she fiddled with the key. "I don't suppose you would want me driving up to Atlanticscape to take you out."

She smiled. "That would give the gossips much food for thought."

"And voice. But you will come again."

"Yes."

"What about the Saturday after I get back? We can go for a drive and a meal across on the mainland. Would you like that?"

Jocelyn said that she would and was letting out the clutch when she realised that she did not know his name. She stopped and looked back over her shoulder to ask him.

"Didn't Cissie tell you?"

"She just mentioned the name of the farm."

His face creased with merriment as he introduced himself, his handshake warm and intimate. "You are Jocelyn something-or-other. I know your name without having to be told."

"Everyone seems to know me and all about me."

"That's Trowsay for you."

She watched him through her rear mirror as she drove off. He stood there for a bit and then turned towards his byre.

When she knew that she was out of sight of the house, Jocelyn stopped the car and rested her forearms along the top of the steering wheel, looking out over the loch but seeing nothing of its changing colour as the sky lightened. Her emotions were in turmoil. It was not just the mourning surrounding Rupert's death that had caused her depressive mood, but seeing and knowing that Thorfinn had merely been flirting with her to pass the time until Hanna was free. She had behaved like an adolescent, reading too much into the fact that he had sought her out as soon as he arrived home from the south and had given her the occasional hug and brief kiss. It was not that he had behaved differently to her after Rupert's death, but now that Hanna was free to give him her full attention, she could witness his devotion; his affection for her had been merely that of a man who liked the company of women, nothing more. She had a feeling that Rab Ballater was the same type. An attractive man who had probably had a series of girl friends before his marriage and was lonely for female company. She was new to the island and it was an advantage that she had not known his wife; she must not read more than that into his invitation out.

A flashing blue light penetrated her inward eye. It was a police car moving at speed along the other side of the loch. She reached over to the glove compartment for her binoculars to see where it was going. It took the turning up to the Selkie Bay farmhouse.

"My goodness!" she exclaimed out loud, stowing the binoculars away and starting the car. She drove at speed along the side of the loch to above the crossing, and was starting along the other side when Davey barred her way forcing her to an abrupt stop.

He scooped up his dog and got into the passenger seat.

"Hurry, now," he wheezed breathlessly, as Heidi

overwhelmed her with hugs and kisses.

"What's happening?" she asked, gently pushing Heidi away.

"I dinna ken yet but we'll ken soon enough."

"The police have turned up the track to Selkie."

"I thocht as much."

"Why?"

Davey chewed away on his teeth while he thought about that.

"There will've been a fight. Mrs. Treatham should never have taken on both Mike and Pete. The families have never got on, and its worse now that Mike has taken a shine to Pete's Mum."

Jocelyn drove on, wondering how she could diffuse any dispute, or even if she had the authority to try. She knew neither man and they might see her as interfering in something that had nothing to do with her.

Davey leaned forward in his seat, clutching Heidi to him.

"There's Mike making a run for it," he exclaimed, drawing her attention to a car that was driving down from the farmhouse at speed, rocking over the potholes. "They'll be after him. Just you wait and see." Despite Davey's certainty, and eagerness to witness a police chase, there was no sign of any car following.

Mike swerved and skidded to a stop beside her at the bottom of the track. His face was flushed and his eyes were bright with excitement.

"We've found a body," he called out from his open window.

Jocelyn stared incredulously.

"We found it underneath the floor in the barn."

"Did you know who it was?"

"Naw. It was just a skeleton, like."

"It winna be a person," Davey said scathingly. "More than likely it'll be an animal of some sort."

Mike leaned back in his seat to survey Davey and give him a malicious grin. He no doubt knew where much of the talk about him and Pete's mother emanated.

"It was an animal all right – an animal with two legs," he sneered, before ignoring him. "It was all crouched up in the hole with its knees touching its chin. I put a spade through it before I realised."

Davey opened his door and let Heidi jump down. "I'll away up and see for myself."

"You winna get past the top of the track," Mike called but Davey kept going. "They've sent for the retired archaeologist from over by to have a look at it before it's moved," he went on, his attention returning to Jocelyn. "The police were saying that there could be religious significance to the way it was buried."

"So it is pre-historic?"

Mike shrugged. "That barn has been standing there for a gie long time."

"Was it deep down?"

"Naw, it wasna that deep."

Jocelyn rubbed the steering wheel in thought before saying: "Mrs. Treatham will be ringing tonight."

"It'll be a right shock for her."

"I think I'll go up and speak to the police and see if they can tell me any more."

"Fine that. And you can tell Hanna when she rings that there will be no more work done this week." He started his car and took off at speed, his tyres screeching and his engine roaring at full throttle.

Davey was sitting on the verge at the top of the track rolling a cigarette, when Jocelyn approached on foot. A blue and white tape was stretched between the two top posts.

"You're not allowed in," he said, closing his tin and putting the skinny cigarette in his mouth.

Jocelyn stayed where she was, wondering what to do. She could not cross the police line but she wanted to know more about the find. There was a female police officer at the entrance to the barn, talking to someone inside, and she decided to make her presence known.

"Hallo, there," she called. Her throat was choked with anxiety and her cry sounded a bit feeble, but the woman turned and scrutinised her. After a moment's hesitation, she walked towards her.

"Are you Mrs. Treatham?" she asked.

"I am a friend of hers," Jocelyn said shyly, putting her hand forward and introducing herself.

The constable took her hand but did not mention her name. She was short with a pear-shaped figure and Jocelyn wondered, momentarily, how someone of her build could subdue a large, intoxicated man.

"Would you ask Mrs. Treatham to come over?"

Jocelyn explained about Hanna being away on holiday and out of touch, adding: "But she telephones every evening to find out how the work is progressing."

"It is at a stop," was the ironic response, made without a change of expression.

"But is there anything I can tell her when she rings?"

The constable looked down at Davey, who was pretending not to be listening, "There is no point in your staying here, Davey," she said.

Davey surveyed the scene in front of him, sucking in his teeth, before answering: "I'm just resting for a while. It's a free country."

"As you like."

The constable obviously knew that any conversation she had there would be repeated, expanded and embroidered to suit Davey's fancy and lifted the tape, allowing Jocelyn in.

"There is nothing that the owner can do at this stage," the constable said when they were out of earshot, "but we will need to contact her."

"She won't be back in Trowsay until next Sunday," Jocelyn told her

"Can you give me her phone number?"

"I'm afraid not. She's on a hiking holiday and camps out."

"I see."

The constable looked thoughtful, which made Jocelyn bold enough to ask if she could be shown what had been found so that she could describe it to Hanna. She had expected a negative response but the constable just shrugged, saying that she did not see any harm in her taking a look.

"We are only here to make sure that no one tampers with the site," she went on, leading the way to the back of the house and the roofless, windowless barn, now joined to the extension. "There has been no recent criminal activity that would provide evidence."

They picked a path over the rubble of cobbles, broken concrete and mud to the far corner where a male constable was erecting a green tent, to protect the burial site from the weather. There was very little to see. The skeleton was only partly exposed, lying on its side with its knees pulled up.

"It has obviously been here for a long time," Jocelyn said, noticing where Mike had thrust his spade down.

Her companion agreed, adding: "We will know how old it is when tests are done."

The male constable gave a last blow with his hammer to the peg he had been inserting into the mud between two cobblestones and rose from his crouched position.

"It may not be as old as we thought originally," he said, kneeling down and lifting a piece of muddy fabric caught underneath the thigh bone.

"Don't pull at it."

"I won't. And there's something else." He pointed to where there was a difference in the colour and texture of the surface round the skeleton and lifted up a piece of concrete to show to his colleague.

She took the piece from him and inspected it, saying to Jocelyn: "I should not have brought you in here." She handed the piece of concrete back and put a hand on Jocelyn's arm to usher her out.

Before Jocelyn turned away, she took a last look at the exposed bones of the skull and the severed shoulder blade embedded in the clinging, red clay. The shape of the skeleton was visible where the soil had been disturbed by the men as they dug, or perhaps, more likely, dragged away with their spades in curiosity. She could see the sharp edges of a split flagstone amongst the chunks of broken concrete at the edge of the hole.

"So the body could have been buried after the barn was built?" she asked as they found their way back over the rubble.

"Everything is only speculation at the moment."

Jocelyn thought about the consequence of finding that the body had been buried within living memory. It could not have been a natural death or it would not have been hidden in that way. On the other hand, nothing happened on Trowsay without everyone knowing.

"Have you any idea when the men can get back to work," she asked as they reached the exit.

"We can't tell at this stage but we'll keep in touch. Mrs. Treatham lives up at Atlanticscape, doesn't she?"

"I live there too."

"All right. Ask her to ring us when you speak to her." She gave the police contact number and rummaged in her pocket for her notebook to pencil down Hanna's details.

"This will cause quite a sensation," Jocelyn commented, turning her head as a gangly youth in an oversized boiler suit appeared beside her.

"Are you still here, Pete?" the constable asked, showing her annoyance.

"Mike went off without me."

"Well, you must be on your way."

"I thocht this wife here might gie me a lift tae the village."

"Mrs. Fenwick."

"Aye, Mrs. Fenwick."

"Of course, I will," Jocelyn said with a smile, to ease Pete's embarrassment at being reprimanded.

"I thocht you might." He held back as the two women walked on, not wanting to crowd them, but when they were at the far side of the courtyard, he started slinking along behind.

"I see that Davey is still here," the constable said.

Jocelyn whispered: "I brought him out, but I don't suppose he wants a lift back along the road. He looks settled for the duration."

But she was wrong. Before she had ducked under the tape and bid the constable good-bye, Davey was on his feet with Heidi dancing around him.

"I was thinking that I needed something for me tea," he said, nodding to Pete and hitching up his trousers. "You'll be going that way?"

Jocelyn said that she was, smiling wryly to herself. She knew why he was leaving. He would get no more information staying where he was, but having her and Pete in the intimate enclosure of her car, would give him ample opportunity to get what he wanted.

"Come on then," she invited, leading the way down the track with Davey and Pete straggling along behind. Jocelyn could hear Davey trying to probe Pete for information but he was monosyllabic in his responses. Heidi was sniffing about in the verges and ditches ahead, and when Davey was settled in the front passenger seat, he gave a sharp whistle, calling her back. It took two whistles before she appeared at the open door and jumped up, panting over her lolling tongue; she eased herself about until she found a stable place for her back paws between Davey's thighs, before resting her front paws on the dashboard.

"That was a right strange thing to find," Davey commented, once the car was purring away nicely.

Jocelyn agreed that it was.

"Did you see it then?" Davey asked, making a more direct approach

Jocelyn said that she had

"And it was a human skeleton?"

"Yes, it was."

"And did it look as if it had been there a long time? Since afore the barn was built, like?"

"I couldn't say," Jocelyn replied diplomatically.

Pete intervened, leaning forward with his forearms resting along the back of their seats: "There were flags o'er the skeleton. We tried heaving them up but they wouldna budge. We had tae split them up wi the pick. It was right hard going."

Jocelyn turned her head slightly to address Pete, whose day's work had taken its toll on his sweat glands. "I noticed that they had been embedded in concrete, not mud."

"Aye, they had."

"Were there flagstones anywhere else in the barn?"

"There wasna. Just cobble maist places and concrete in the stalls."

"Well, what do you make of a' that?" Davey asked, mystified.

"It isna an ancient burial site and the body wasna there since afore the barn was built," Pete stated with certainty.

"Well, now, is that a fact!" Davey cogitated for a bit, chewing on his mouth; he dropped the top set of his teeth on to the bottom set with a click before replacing them with his tongue. "That farm was aye in the Maconachie family, passed down frae fether tae son, it was."

"I ken that. But they're a' deed noo."

"Maybe so but they were a respected family up there at Selkie. At least they were afore that sharp-faced, bigoted wife was brought home from over by."

Jocelyn smiled. "I don't think her religious inclination has anything to do with it, Davey."

"Maybe no but we canna be doing with that sort of thing hereabouts. You should ask Flo McFea about the wife. She bided there when she was a bairn."

"How long ago was that?"

"A piece back. In the thirties like."

Pete gave a low whistle, lifting a hand to push his glasses back up his nose. The bridge between the lenses had been repaired with a piece of elastoplast. "That's a fair time ago. She micht ken somethin."

"Aye, she might."

Davey had been given food for thought and was silent as they rounded the end of the loch. But he wasn't silent for long.

"I saw you comin down frae Shaws," he commented as they were passing Rab Ballater's road end. He glanced sideways inquisitively but Jocelyn did not rise to the bait. "Is he fine enough?"

"Cissie asked me to deliver his groceries."

"Is that a fact!"

She hoped that neither man had noticed her heated face or had not interpreted anything from it, but Davey's response and subsequent silence spoke volumes. She hated to be the subject of gossip but when she dropped them off in the village, there was a jaunty swing to Davey's step as he followed Heidi up to the shop door. The sort of jaunty step which bespoke of his having two pieces of news to spread thickly over the island.

9

The house was still unlit and empty when Bill got home next time. The abundant use of cleaning fluid had left a stale odour, which was mixed with the mustiness of an unaired house. The central heating was on low but he shivered, feeling the cold sweat of sickness engulf him. Jo had been absent for more than five weeks without a word of explanation. Something had happened to her. It couldn't be an accident; she would have had identification in her handbag. He did not want to consider the alternative but it still forced its way into his thoughts. She had been abducted, raped and murdered.

The police were less dismissive this time but they did not jump to the same conclusion as he had done. They reiterated the known facts: she had left home to visit her mother; her mother no longer lived at the flat where she had lived up until a year or two before. The desk sergeant advised Bill to speak to the mother's neighbours in the tenement block and if they could not help him, to look in the Electoral Register for that area or contact the social work department at Dundee council. He made a note of the fact that Jo had been reported missing but pointed out that missing people sometimes did not want to be found. Bill assured him that his relationship with Jo was close and that that would not be the case with her.

The next day he spent hours on the phone following up the suggestions that had been made, but he got frustrated with pressing buttons, listening to inane music and being transferred from this taped message to that without success. In the end he decided to go back up to Dundee, speak to the neighbours first, and then check the records himself.

He arrived at the tenement block in the early afternoon, threading his way through a rambling crowd of idle shoppers and mothers with prams, moving in both directions. Outside the building, cars and lorries were packed together, their engines turning over idly and emitting hot exhaust fumes; when the lights lazily changed to green, the solid mass surged forward with rising acceleration. Bad enough to live in a city, Bill thought, as he opened the outside door, but hell to have a flat overlooking street lights.

Inside the building there was a heavy, slumbering silence, only broken by the resonance of his footsteps as he climbed to the top floor. There was no response there to his long press on each doorbell, but on the floor below, an attractive middle-aged woman in a loosely tied dressing-grown, took his hand and drew him into her flat. She was babbling away about something as she pulled him across her hall towards a half-open door. He was so stunned to find himself taking part in what he had always considered to be a sexual fantasy, he wasn't paying any attention to what she was saying, so when he found himself in a bathroom rather than a bedroom, his brain was still whirling along the same lines; he was wondering if she had some sexual fixation about bathrooms. However instead of clutching him to her partly exposed bosom, she was pointing to a leggy spider trapped on the porcelain surface of the bath. He could not take it in for a moment and then he chortled, gently lifting the frightened, scuttling arachnid on to the outside window ledge. He turned from closing the window, hoping that this request was just a prelude to better things, but he found her gratitude to be wordily profuse rather than sexually demonstrative. The whole episode had taken less than twenty seconds and it was all so bizarre, he was amused rather than disappointed when he found himself back on the landing.

He hadn't even had time to ask her about Jo's mother.

The only other person at home in the building was an old man who had been woken up from his afternoon sleep by the ringing of his door bell. The expression in his bleary eyes quickly changed to anger when he heard why he had been disturbed. He told Bill, in blistering language, that he kept himself to himself and had nothing to do with nosey neighbours or strangers who had no consideration for others. Bill would normally have given as good as he got but he was still reflecting upon his encounter upstairs. He knew that it would make a good pub story, even without embellishment.

At the council offices, he found that Jo's mother was not in sheltered housing and she was not under the care of the social services. She was also no longer on the Electoral Register. The official in this latter office pointed out that she could have moved out of their area and Bill waited, biting his lip, while she consulted her computer

"Mrs. Simpson was registered at 11 Lower Commercial Road until 1995," she read from her screen.

"Can you see where she went after that?"

There was a lot more key tapping.

"There's no record of her at any other address in our area. She could have passed on, of course."

"Passed on? Passed on where?"

The woman put her elbows along the front of her desk and glanced up at him over the top of her spectacles, without expression or comment.

"You mean died?" Bill dismissed this suggestion with a flick of his wrist. "I wouldn't be here asking about her, if she had died."

"Well, there you are. I can't help you any further."

Bill mumbled an automatic thanks and was at the door when the official called: "She could have remarried."

"She's an elderly wife."

"It happens."

He lost his way in the labyrinth of corridors while trying to find his way back to the front reception desk, and passed a sign and an arrow pointing in the direction of the Registrar of Births, Marriages and Deaths. It seemed an extraordinary coincidence to find himself in that part of the building and although he felt sure that it was a waste of time making enquiries there, he had plenty of time and no where to go.

There were two women in front of him, holding sleeping babies in their arms. They eyed him speculatively when he came in, no doubt assuming that he was a new father; but he gave nothing away. He just nodded in their direction while he unzipped his anorak, and slumped down on a vacant seat, with a leg thrust out. They tried to include him in their animated and intimate conversation but he kept his head partly turned away, listening to what they had to say, but only occasionally swivelling his eyes in their direction.

When it was his turn to be attended to, a gaunt, young man with receding hair and tired eyes called him through.

He gave Bill a loose handshake and invited him to sit down, taking his place behind the desk. He was already aware that Bill was not there to register a birth and he had the appropriate ledger on his desk.

"You're wondering if this Mrs. Simpson remarried within the last couple of years. Is that right?" he asked.

Bill said that it was.

"There is no record of it, I'm afraid." He tapped the ledger beside him to emphasize the point. "But let me see now." He began to thump away on the keys of his computer, repeating Bill's limited information. He finished typing, read his screen and started again; then he got up and replaced the heavy ledger on his desk with another and tracked down the entries with his fingers. He was about to speak to Bill but changed his mind, going over to open a filing cabinet and rifle through the files with his fingers. He consulted a folder as he walked back to the counter.

"It is Elizabeth Venetia Simpson of 11 Lower Commercial Road you're trying to trace?"

Bill said that it was.

"I'm sorry," the man apologised, glancing up at Bill and then down at a form in his folder, "but Mrs. Simpson died on 14th September 1996."

"She can't have."

"She did."

It was shattering news and he could hardly take it in Jo had visited her mother at least three times in the previous year. If she hadn't been going there, and obviously she hadn't, where had she been going. His original disbelief was followed by bewilderment and then anger. He might be a bit untidy around the house but he loved her and he was not an ogre. There was no need for her to lie to him.

He exited the building and crossed the road without noticing that the lights were still at green and nearly got knocked down by a bus. He lifted two fingers in response to the sustained hoot of the horn and was momentarily uplifted by the driver's reaction, supported by the outrage of his mostly elderly female passengers, sitting along the near side of the bus. He went into the pub at the next corner and ordered a pint. There were only two other drinkers there, creeping soaks at either end of the counter, and he drank his pint in silence, shrugging off an attempt to get him into conversation. He drained his glass and was on his way back to the railway station.

As the train swayed south, he turned the pages of a motor cycle magazine but he could not concentrate. Jo had been living a double life and he could not face the possibility that she might have been visiting a lover. Thinking about that, reminded him of the woman in the dressing grown. He could not really believe that she would answer the doorbell, partly naked, and invite a strange man into her flat only to remove an innocuous spider. She had wanted him to flush it down the toilet but he had opened the window and put it out instead. Perhaps that was where he had gone wrong. She feared it would come right back in. He could not imagine anyone being overly frightened of a non-stinging, non-biting insect. His father had taught him to be curious about all the creatures they found in the garden and had held them in his hand for him to touch and examine when he was a small boy. His thoughts shifted to that time, before he started school and before his parents had had an ill-tempered separation; automatically he reached into his pocket for his cigarettes and had the temporary pleasure of ignoring the self-righteous expression of the man sitting opposite who pointed out the No Smoking sign. The ensuing diatribe ended with the guard being called and threatening to put him off at the next station.

When he got home, the ansaphone was flicking red, but he did not stop in the hall, knowing that it would be one of Jo's friends. He was fed up at having to listen to their barely veiled condemnation.

He threw his anorak down at the bottom of the stairs and went through to the kitchen to put a frozen pizza in the microwave, thinking how different it would be if Jo had been there preparing a decent meal and asking about his day. He tried to summon up the sound and smell of meat roasting in the oven but without success; but he could visualise Jo bending down to open the oven door and lift the sizzling pan up on to the hob. She had a lovely arse. He closed his eyes and leaned against the table as the image developed into a full blown fantasy, but it was soon over and he was once more beset with despair. He took some beers from the fridge and slouched through to the sittingroom, feeling maudlin.

None of it was his fault. It was others who had dictated the direction of his life; Jo's rejection and their separation was part of that pattern. Why couldn't she remember how it had been when they first met and allow him to rekindle the flame.

After eating, he dozed for a bit in front of the television, but he couldn't get Jo's desertion out of his thoughts. His emotions went the full circle. Anger reasserted itself but then it gave way to dismay and back to despair. In the end, he decided to employ a private detective to find her. The Yellow Pages were on the shelf underneath the telephone and he went through to the hall to get the directory. The red light on the ansaphone was still flashing, demanding attention, and he pressed 'play' in irritation, sure that it would be one of Jo's friends, plaguing him with questions that he could not answer.

He was knocked back when he heard Jo's voice.

"Bill, I just wanted you to know that I am safe and well," he heard her say and his legs gave way. He sat down on the stairs in shock.

"Where are you?" he asked over the continuation of the message.

"I don't know when I will be returning home but I am sure you will manage. The house insurance needs to be renewed this month. Would you see to it? I'll keep in touch. Bye."

It told him everything and nothing. He still did not know where she was.

10

Hanna did not telephone in the early evening as she usually did.

"She must have had an accident," Phil said tensely, pouring a glass of wine for Jocelyn. His bulky shoulders were slumped and his brow furrowed with anxiety.

"It's far more likely that there are no telephones near their camp site," Jocelyn replied gently, taking the drink and sitting down beside Bridget at the kitchen table. As there were only the three of them left, it was cosier to sit with Phil in the kitchen.

"But she said last night that they were going to book into a hotel in Lairg," Phil said

Bridget agreed.

"The weather could have improved and they have decided to camp after all," Jocelyn said, in an effort to reassure him.

"Or perhaps she thinks that missing a night doesn't matter," Bridget put in. "We haven't had much news for her up until now."

Phil lifted the pasta pan off the hot plate, holding the lid on with an oven glove. "She would want to know about the discovery."

"If she doesn't know about it, she can't fret."

"And she can enjoy the rest of her holiday," Jocelyn added.

Phil nodded, accepting the logic of this, as he tipped the pan over the sink and drained the water off. He put a sizeable mound of pasta on each plate, covering this with steaming spaghetti sauce. "Help yourselves to Parmesan," he invited, putting the pan on the side and sitting down at the head of the table. The parmesan was passed to him and he sprinkled a liberal amount over his spaghetti, before cutting it into tiny bits and spooning it into his mouth. It was a very sensible way to tackle the dish, Jocelyn thought, as she bit off the surplus from her straggly mouthful. She wished she could manage to twirl it round her fork successfully like Bridget who could make neat bundles, enclosing the sauce. Jocelyn wondered if she had Italian genes as well as Irish blood.

"Perhaps she'll ring later," Phil said, as much to comfort himself as to communicate his thoughts.

They agreed and the silence lengthened. Jocelyn was very conscious of the ticking of the wall clock. It was one of Phil's creations based on Hickory Dickory Dock. There was a mouse with a very long tail running up the clock stem but there was also a menagerie of other animals and garden birds watching it from different places round the mounting. She had commented on it before, indicating her delight with the detail, but it now prompted her to ask Phil if he had really only started doing sculptures after meeting Duncan.

"I was always good with my hands," Phil told her, "and I made things for my mother from an early age."

"She must have been very proud of your talent."

Phil chuckled. "I suppose she was. The first wooden sculpture I made for her was a flying swan with wings that fluttered up and down when the battery was turned on. She put it in the vestibule so that she could point it out to strangers who came to the house."

"Did you have any brothers or sisters?"

"No, there were only the two of us." He put his spoon and fork down and sat back in his chair. "She had a hard life, my Mum, working all hours and earning only a pittance."

"What happened to your Dad?" Bridget asked, with an enquiring glance.

"He was killed in the war before I was born."

"Didn't the two families rally round her?"

"Nawp." Phil picked up his fork and started to mess around with his spaghetti. "She was an unmarried mother," he told them, adding, with an ironic smile: "That put a stain on her character."

"How dreadful!" Jocelyn exclaimed.

Phil shrugged. "That was how it was then. My loving, hard-working Mum was considered to be a slut, although she told me that she had never been with any other man."

"Thank goodness that doesn't happen nowadays."

"There will still be a stigma, I assure you."

"And you, Phil, how did it effect you?"

"I was a bastard."

"That's a cruel word to use."

"But that was the word that was used to describe children like me." He lifted up his wine glass and drank. "I used to spend my free time down at the youth club and was encouraged to take up weightlifting. Physical strength has its plus side when you are being taunted, although I never wanted to fight."

"You were good at the sport though," Jocelyn said, with a smile. There were photographs of Phil, lifting weights and receiving cups or written tributes, on the walls of the downstairs loo. She had studied these. "You won a county championship."

"I enjoyed practising and competing but I was too busy earning a living to keep it up later."

"Was Duncan a weightlifter too?" Bridget asked. .

Phil laughed. "Nothing like that. He was small and skinny when I first met him."

"I never pictured him like that. How did you meet?"

Phil did not immediately respond to Bridget's curiosity. He looked at her reflectively as if he was wondering how much to tell. Her response to Rupert and Hanna's unorthodox marriage had made him wary of giving her access to his intimate life. Eventually he said: "Duncan came to my workshop wanting a special frame made for one of his large paintings."

"And you never looked back."

"You could say that." He turned to Jocelyn. "Thanks for getting the shopping. Normally I enjoy going down to the village and passing the time of day with Cissie or the fishermen at the pier, but my mind was engrossed."

"I'm always pleased to do these things for you," Jocelyn told him, lifting her napkin and dabbing some of the spaghetti sauce off her chin. "By the way, my battery was flat and I took a jump from your landrover. I didn't want to disturb you again to ask."

"No trouble."

"Sometimes my boot doesn't close properly and runs it down."

"I'll have a look at it for you. Did you find the charger?"

"Yes, I've put it on charge but Ted Vale says that I need a new battery."

"Is he getting you one?"

"Yes. He'll have it here by tomorrow. It's amazing what they've got down there. I even saw a meat safe and I can't imagine who would want such a thing when everyone has fridges nowadays."

Phil chuckled "They are still used."

"For what?"

"For grouse and hare. I have one in the courtyard. I'll point it out to you. I don't shoot myself but I'm often given limp presents and hook them up inside there until they mature."

"Sounds disgusting."

"Not if you don't leave them too long and they are delicious to eat." He lifted his wine glass. "Was Cissie saying anything of interest?"

Jocelyn gave a light laugh. "Most of it I would not repeat." She was not going to tell him that Hanna's relationships and financial prospects had been Cissie's main topic of conversation.

"Even to me."

"Best not."

"Quite right." He pushed the rest of his spaghetti to the side and mopped up a pool of spilled wine. "What about you, Bridget? What have you been up to?"

"I spent most of the morning at the hotel making sure that everything was ready for my window. Thorfinn can help me take it down when he comes back."

"I could help you."

"It's heavy."

Phil gave a crooked smile. "I'm not decrepit yet."

"Thanks for offering but I told Jean Glover that it would be early next week and she is going to have the handyman standing by." She turned to Jocelyn. "Have you met Jean Glover, the manageress at the hotel?"

Jocelyn said that she had.

"She's very helpful," Bridget commented, reaching for her wine glass. "I discussed with her ideas for the window on the other side of the porch and did rough sketches for her to see, but a decision will not be taken locally, which seems absurd."

"The hotel is part of the Verity chain now. Perhaps you'll get commissions for their hotels south."

Bridget hadn't thought of that and brightened up. "Jean was telling me that they're having a ceilidh there soon to celebrate the first day of summer. Will we go?"

"Certainly we'll go."

"Will it really be summer?"

"According to the calendar."

Phil offered more spaghetti but this was refused and they sat over their empty plates while he reminisced about island ceilidhs that he had attended in the past, where romances prospered and scores were settled.

"Everyone attends from the greatest grand-parent to the smallest toddler," he told them, "and the presence of the extended family keeps the disputes and drinkers in check. It wasn't Duncan's scene but he always wanted me to go and….." He stopped in mid-sentence, hearing distant voices calling from through the house. "They're back," he exclaimed in surprise and delight, pushing back his chair and getting up.

Slavers bounded through to greet them and Phil bent to accept his embraces, looking up as Hanna came in. Her wan and distracted look had gone and her distinctive honey-coloured beauty was enhanced by glowing cheeks.

There was laughter and hugs all round.

"Where's Thorfinn?" Phil asked.

"He's here."

Thorfinn came in with a ta-ra. There was something concealed under his anorak which undulated with irregular movement. As they watched, a head appeared, a white doggie head with black patched eyes, floppy black ears and large frightened eyes.

"Bernie the second," Thorfinn said, unzipping his anorak and lifting the St. Bernard puppy into Phil's uncertain arms.

Slavers came over to sniff and wag his tail at the fluffy puppy's closed rear end, as it scratched at Phil's shirt front with its large short-clawed paws, wriggling to be free. Phil set it down and went over to the sink to pour some water into a bowl for the puppy to drink.

"Bernie the fourth," he said quietly, still bewildered by the unexpected gift. He murmured thanks, coming back with the full bowl of water and setting it down for Bernie to drink. The puppy put as much water on the floor as in its mouth, looking up at Phil as it licked. Drinking rather than sucking was obviously a new experience. "I thought I was too old for another dog."

"He will always have a second home with us," Hanna said, taking Phil's hand and looking up into his eyes to impress her sincerity.

The puppy finished drinking and Hanna went to get some kitchen paper to mop up the spills while Phil lifted the puppy up into his arms. It rested its head against his shoulder and yawned.

"We weren't expecting you until Sunday," Phil said, gesturing to the chairs round the table and sitting down with Bernie on his lap.

"We had to come back when we heard the news."

"What news?"

"Haven't you heard? They've found a skeleton in the barn over at Selkie."

"We know that, but how did you know?"

Hanna laughed. "By a long circuitous route. Mike called in at the hotel for a drink on his way home…."

"Our hotel?"

"Yes…..and Jean Glove telephoned her mother; she rang her elder daughter in Inverness, who works with a man whose wife has connections with the hotel in Lairg where we were going to stay. There may have been other 'in betweens' but that is the gist of it."

"Incredible."

"But inevitable," Thorfinn remarked pithily, adding with a chuckle: "Davey was very put out that he was not the first to give us the news. He saw us coming and was up on the road in a flash to wave us down."

Phil stroked his new Bernie, soothing his qualms, while Jocelyn told them about giving Davey a lift that afternoon. She went on to describe her meeting with the police and the scraped-back hole where the skeleton lay.

"We were told that it was an ancient burial site and that more skeletons would be found," Hanna said, when Jocelyn had finished bringing them up-to-date, "but Davey implied that the Maconachies had buried the body there."

"After committing some foul deed," Thorfinn added, passing a finger across his throat dramatically.

"Is that true?" Hanna asked Jocelyn.

Jocelyn laughed. "Davey is guessing but he may have

been guessing correctly in this instance. They cannot tell how old the bones are until tests are done, but there was new concrete in the area."

"Is that significant?"

"Possibly. Equally important, they found a piece of cloth underneath one of the thigh bones."

"Did they now!"

Thorfinn chuckled and began to put forward far-fetched possibilities, such as the skeleton being that of a travelling atheist that Mrs. Maconachie had thought it her duty to exterminate, or a lady of the night who had answered Alec's silent, frustrated call and succumbed to his deadly embraces.

"If you say things like that outside these four walls, Thorfinn," Hanna reprimanded gently, "They will be taken seriously."

"What fun!"

Bridget said drolly: "It sounds as if this family had a skeleton or two in their cupboard as well as in their barn."

"Don't listen to Thorfinn, Bridget. He is being unkind. I liked Alec. There was no harm in him."

"He used to ask me if I had any soft porn magazines," Thorfinn mused.

"And did you have?" Bridget asked with mock innocence, which was answered with a chortle from Thorfinn and a measuring stare from Hanna.

"He also wondered if I had any illegal drugs because he wanted to give them a try."

"And did you have?" Bridget repeated, unabashed by Hanna's displeasure.

"Don't encourage him, Bridget."

Thorfinn laughed, adding: "According to Davey, the

mysterious skeleton was not the only gossip doing the rounds." He glanced sideways at Jocelyn.

Hanna hushed him and he subsided ostentatiously.

Jocelyn tried to brazen it out by looking blank, but she was aware of eyes turning towards her and wished that she did not blush so easily. A widening circle of gossips might know about her delivering groceries to Shaws but no one could know about her emotional meeting with Rab, if she showed no reaction.

"So what have you been up to, Jocelyn?" Bridget asked.

"I have no idea. Ask Thorfinn."

"No, don't ask Thorfinn," Hanna interrupted. "He knows, as well as everyone else, that Davey's talk is based on very little substance." She made a dismissive gesture and changed the subject.

While they were speaking, Phil had got up and gone through to the scullery with the sleepy Bernie still in his arms. He came back with a flat vegetable basket and a stone hot-water bottle which he proceeded to fill from the kettle on the side of the Aga. He wrapped it in a towel and laid the puppy gently down in the basket close to the bottle. Once the puppy was settled and reassured, Phil turned to the task of feeding the travellers and hearing all about their holiday.

11

"He was too young to leave his mother," were Phil's first words when he came into the kitchen the next morning, Bernie curled in his arms. He put him down on the polished flagstones and he bounded around with wagging tail, greeting everyone. Slavers pulled himself up from his usual place close to the Aga and stood watching him paternally.

"Did you have a disturbed night?" Hanna asked anxiously, getting up to put the kettle on and make fresh tea.

"He wouldn't settle," Phil responded dolefully. "I took him up on to my bed but he was still restless and I had to come down and boil some milky water. How old is he?"

"He would've been seven weeks if we had collected him on Sunday."

"That is far too young to leave his mother. I wonder if he would take baby milk from a bottle."

"He is weaned," Hanna said, pouring hot water into the tea pot, "and we brought the right sort of puppy food."

"You can leave him with us tonight, Phil," Thorfinn offered, watching Bernie sniffing along the skirting board. "Give you a rest."

"No, I can't do that. He is just getting to know me."

"Isn't he delightful," Bridget exclaimed watching the puppy's progress round the room. Bernie's response to her words was to squat and do what came naturally. This brought smiles and chuckles all round and Thorfinn got up to clean the mess.

"There's a pile of newspapers in the cupboard, Thorfinn," Phil instructed, as Hanna fussed over him, pouring a cup of strong tea and making fresh toast. "Would you put a wad of them on that spot? We will try and get him to use the same place although we can't expect miracles for a good few weeks." He drank deeply, the strong brew hitting his stomach and reviving his spirits. "You make a good cup of tea, Hanna."

"It's the least I can do." She took his hand and pressed it affectionately, before starting to clear the dirty dishes off the table. Thorfinn crouched at the dishwasher, ready to load them in as she handed them down. "We're off across to Selkie to see what's going on. Is there anything you would like me to get at the shop?"

"No, I'll go across to Tongue later. I might be able to get a proper basket and other odds and ends for Bernie there."

"We could do that."

"No, leave it to me."

Bridget waylaid Thorfinn as he was leaving the kitchen, to ask if he would carry her window down to the hotel on Monday. Jocelyn could hear Thorfinn's banter about being the first to be allowed to see it, before their voices faded.

"I'll have another cup of tea," she said, reaching for the teapot and pouring half a cup before getting up for the kettle to dilute it to the strength she liked.

"What do you think you'll be up to today?" Phil asked.

Jocelyn shrugged. "I haven't thought about it yet." She had no fixed schedule and was pleased to just sit there and keep Phil company.

"Coo-ee," came from through the house, followed by clicking steps moving at speed along the corridor to the kitchen. It was Patsy Gunn's day for coming in to do the cleaning.

"I see they're back," she said as she reached the kitchen door, stopping abruptly when she saw Bernie. "Well, I never! What has the cat brought in? I didn't know you were getting another dog, Phil. Well I never! He's a fine looking specimen, I must say. Or is he a she?"

Slavers and Bernie were competing to give her a warm welcome which had created bedlam.

"Good morning, Patsy," Phil said, getting a word in while he had a chance.

"He's a he," Patsy said, lifting Bernie up to have a closer look. "Just what you needed, Phil, a new dog to keep your mind off your fancy ideas."

Phil glanced in Jocelyn's direction and she smiled. She knew that she was one of his fancy ideas.

"There you are now," Patsy went on, putting Bernie down and petting Slavers to show him that he was not forgotten. "We can't be letting this newcomer put your nose out of joint, can we, my pet?"

When Patsy had finished giving Slavers verbal reassurance, Phil said: "I'm afraid he'll be making a few messes but I'll keep my eye out for them."

Patsy shrugged that off as being natural. "We'll get him trained between us," she went on, going into the scullery to collect her bits and pieces. As she only came in twice a week, it was unlikely that she would be taking any part in his training but she liked to feel part of the households where she worked. "I'll give Jason's room a good going over," she went on, coming out and heading for the door. "No word of him coming back?"

"He won't be back."

"Not surprising, if you want my opinion. I have never seen the likes of the rubbish he produced up there. I'll clear the lot out."

She was off. Patsy was never idle; she was a great talker but her tongue worked on the move. When she had finished her hours at Atlanticscape, she would be back to the Manse to see to Martha Silver, the minister's sister who was an invalid, and then on to the hotel to work in the kitchen over lunchtime. On Mondays she would fit Davey into her schedule. He was her Grandad and she tried to keep his caravan spic and span, as well as his person.

After her footsteps had faded into the distance, Phil put his mug down and rested his elbows on the table. He looked down at the sturdy, thick-coated Bernie where he lay on the rug beside the Aga. Slavers had gone off with Patsy and the puppy had wriggled forward to stretch out on the favoured spot.

"They meant well," he said, "and I have been missing old Bernie's company, but I don't know if I will be able to lift this one when he gets old or ill."

Jocelyn murmured sympathetically.

"And it was Duncan who took my dogs for their daily walk."

"Thorfinn is a walker."

"But he's south for most of the week and they will have their own place soon."

Jocelyn could see the anxiety lines deepening on Phil's face as he thought of all the difficulties ahead.

"Would you like me to take him for a walk today?"

she asked gently.

"He won't be able to walk far yet," Phil warned her.

"I'll make a sling and carry him when he gets tired."

"A puppy needs a lot of looking after."

"I know. You go back upstairs and get on. I will see to him."

As soon as Phil was on his feet, Bernie was awake, lolloping around and yelping with exuberance, demanding attention. Phil bent and picked him up.

"I'll take him with me just now."

"All right. Let me get finished and then I'll collect him."

It was a warm but hazy day, when Jocelyn set out on her walk towards the coast, Bernie's short legs and irregular movements hither and thither making her progress slow. Fortunately the fine veil of moisture was slowly evaporating, the lifting shroud brightening with rays of coloured sunlight. In the distance the houses on the outskirts of the village were appearing and disappearing in the swirling mist, and she was wondering how that effect could be rendered in paint when she heard Bernie yelping. He had jumped through a space in one of the derelict greenhouses and was standing there motionless, surrounded by broken glass and spiky wood. Her heart leapt with anxiety.

"Stay," she commanded in a loud voice and Bernie slumped down, his eyes wide with terror. She eased herself through a jagged space, extricating her anorak from a prominent nail. He backed away, his body low. She knelt down, speaking to him in a gentle, soothing voice, and he came towards her very slowly. When he was within reaching distance, she scooped him up and held him close. Once outside, she sat down in the budding heather and inspected all his paws. He did not seem to have been cut and she sighed with relief.

"You gave me quite a fright," she scolded as she manipulated him into the safety of the sling that she had made from a bath sheet, feeling the weighty warmth of his body tugging at her neck muscles. He stuck his head out and looked up at her with soft, appealing eyes, in which she read an apology. "All right; I'll lift you down as soon as we are clear of this debris," she told him, watching her step as she followed the meandering path towards the folly. He was surprisingly heavy and she was glad to release him. The short rest had restored his high spirits and he was off, running between the heather and sheep-soured grass. With the drying of the air and the dissolving of the clouds, sea birds, nesting on the cliffs ahead, were leaving their precarious perches and rising up, swooping and calling as they set off out to sea to forage for food.

She sat down near the folly and Bernie slumped down facing her, his eyes closing in fatigue. Phil was right. He couldn't manage to walk far yet, but his stillness and position was an opportunity for her to attempt a drawing. It was difficult for her to imagine this fluffy bundle as a fully grown St. Bernard. He had the solid build, but his panda-like markings with black-patched eyes, floppy black ears and smooth white fur running down his muzzle to the tip of his shiny nose, did not seem to evoke the St. Bernards that she had seen in the past. She took out her sketch pad and was totally absorbed until she heard the shriek of an oyster-catcher. She saw it some distance away alternating quick wing-beats and strident calls with walking and lop-sided flapping, giving the impression that one of its wings was broken. She knew that this was a ploy to lead any intruder away from its nest, but she could see no one from where she was sitting and presumed that it was just a straying sheep that had caused the disturbance. She went back to work, her attention once more focused on the sleeping dog, and so was startled to be addressed by Thorfinn close at hand.

He came towards her from the shore road.

"My goodness, where did you spring from?" she asked, shutting her sketch pad and slipping it into her pocket.

Their voices had woken Bernie and he was up and yelping around Thorfinn's trouser legs to get attention; Thorfinn played chasing games with him for a bit before dropping down beside Jocelyn and pulling the puppy close.

"Aren't you going to allow me to see?" Thorfinn asked, with a nod towards her pocket.

"I can't draw animals and wouldn't have attempted it had I thought anyone was around."

"Am I 'anyone' now, Jocelyn," Thorfinn enquired, looking hurt. "You always let me see your drawings in the past."

Jocelyn smiled but she did not take her pad out of her pocket. "How did you get here?" she asked.

"I walked round the coast."

"From Selkie Bay? That must be miles."

"About three miles probably."

"Where is Hanna?"

"When I left her, she was still outside the police tape at the bottom of the Selkie track. Half the island was there, agog with curiosity."

"But Hanna is different from the others. Surely they could have let her up to the house."

"We thought so, especially as the black van had been and taken the skeleton away, but nothing doing. You were lucky to get through yesterday before it was sealed off."

"I suppose I was. Perhaps they blame me for initiating the gossip."

"No one initiates gossip on Trowsay. It is in the air we breathe." He broke off a piece of grass and started sucking it. "The local cops just succumbed to your charm."

Jocelyn ignored the intended flattery. She could still feel his attraction but she knew now that it meant nothing. He was just flirting with her.

"Hanna must be annoyed to be excluded."

"It takes a lot to annoy Hanna but she was getting a bit scratchy, so I thought I would just leave her to it."

Jocelyn glanced down at him where he lay, resting on an elbow. She had always admired his easy-going manner and had not dwelt on his faults, but she knew that it was mental cowardice to transfer the burden of life's unpleasantness on to the shoulders of someone else. To 'leave Hanna to it' was typical of Thorfinn.

"What are you thinking about?" Thorfinn asked.

She smiled, pausing before saying: "I was just wondering what they were up to over there at Selkie."

"Everyone is wondering."

"Perhaps they're digging up more bodies?"

"Or making sure that there are no more." He sat up and took Bernie on his knee. "So what do you think of Rab Ballater?"

"What do you mean?" Jocelyn asked quickly, startled

by the unexpected question.

Thorfinn chuckled and said softly: "Lovely Jocelyn, you blush most beautifully."

"I only delivered his shopping."

"And stayed for lunch."

"How could you possibly know that?"

"Cissie knew when you left the shop and Davey saw you coming down from Shaws. They could work it out from that; no doubt adding on an hour or two."

Jocelyn could see that she was defeated and gave in. "He is rather nice," she confided, with a soft reminiscent smile. "Tell me about him. I know about his wife."

"I'll tell you on the way back." Thorfinn lifted Bernie off his knee and put him down gently on his paws before getting to his feet. He pulled Jocelyn up and she stumbled against him, but he didn't take advantage of her close proximity as he would have done in the past. He had grasped that her attitude to him had changed.

"He's a great guy," Thorfinn began, as they started up the meandering path, avoiding the slippery, muddy places and rabbit scrapes, "one of the boys until Ursula tied him down."

"Perhaps he wanted to be 'tied down'."

"Assuredly he did. As soon as Ursula appeared on the scene, he was lost to his mates and the happy bachelor life."

"And what is 'the happy bachelor life', may I ask?

Thorfinn laughed and put his arm lightly across Jocelyn's shoulders, but she wriggled free, saying severely: "You may still be trying to enjoy 'the happy bachelor life', Thorfinn, but you are spoken for."

He chuckled. "Indeed I am." He reached down to lift Bernie up. "Let me take that sling from you, Jocelyn," he offered, holding Bernie on one shoulder. "He's a heavy lump." Once Bernie was stowed away, he went on with his narrative: "Rab inherited Shaws from some relation or other about six years ago and came over here from the wilds of Canada to farm. He hadn't farmed before …

"No, he was a mountie."

"A mountie! Is that what he told you?" Thorfinn looked down at Jocelyn with amusement. "I can see that Rab still knows how to impress the opposite sex."

"Wasn't he a mountie?"

"I've no idea. He was in the police force, but he probably travelled around in a car rather than on a high horse wearing a fancy uniform."

Jocelyn smiled. "I can just picture him up on a horse. But I'll settle for the farming image."

"So you are going to settle for him?"

"Of course not." They walked in silence for a bit and then Jocelyn said ruefully: "I like it here but I have commitments at home and must go back and sort things out some time soon. Besides that, I cannot abuse Phil's hospitality much longer."

"He likes having you here. I can tell."

"It's make-believe."

Bernie wriggled to be free, seeing the derelict greenhouses and sensing adventure, but Jocelyn told Thorfinn about their escapade on the way down and he distracted the puppy by changing his position.

"I still have my bachelor pad," Thorfinn told her "Hanna and I used to stay there when we came up on holiday, but I can't see her leaving Atlanticscape until we move into the farmhouse."

"Are you offering it for rent?"

"I might even sell it."

"What sort of place is it?"

"Just a living room with bedroom and bathroom. It's at this side of Selkie Bay."

"I'll think about it."

"Let me show you it sometime."

"No commitment."

"No commitment."

Hanna was getting out of her car as they were leaving the shrubbery and was none too pleased to see them crossing the gravelled forecourt together.

"I waited for you," she said, looking across at Thorfinn and then sliding a glance towards Jocelyn. "I thought you were only walking across the hill to visit Mrs. McFea."

"Sorry about that, my lovely," Thorfinn said, putting an arm across her shoulders and pulling her close. "Mrs. McFea wasn't in and so I decided that I might as well walk on."

Hanna was not mollified.

"You are as thoughtless as Rupert was," she said, walking out of his arms and turning towards the front door.

"Hanna, darling!" Thorfinn exclaimed in distress, following her. "Don't be like that." He had to stop to lift Bernie down and by the time he straightened up, he was facing a closed door. "Why was she so angry?" he asked Jocelyn, taking the sling off and handing it to her, but he did not wait for a reply.

Jocelyn followed Bernie up the two shallow steps slowly. She knew why Hanna was upset. She had had a frustrating morning and to see Thorfinn ambling up happily in her company was the last straw. She must know that Thorfinn had a wandering eye and that he would have been flirting with her, but what could she say to dispel that thought. She couldn't voice her innocence without making matters worse.

When she opened the inner door, she found them still in the hall, waiting for her.

"I'm sorry, Jocelyn," Hanna said, kissing her on the cheek. Jocelyn could see that the fire inside her had not completely settled; her cheeks were still hot and the spark in her eyes had not been extinguished, but obviously she was not going to let a quarrel mar the harmony in Phil's house.

"I was glad to meet up with Thorfinn on my walk," Jocelyn consoled, hoping that that would stress the extent of their contact. "I had gone too far and didn't realise that Bernie was so heavy to carry."

"Good."

"What is going on over at Selkie Bay?" she ventured as Hanna turned towards the stairs.

"Who knows? The skeleton is no longer there but they still won't let anyone through."

"Perhaps they are collecting evidence."

"Perhaps." She started to climb the stairs. "I'll see you at lunch."

Thorfinn followed her, with a sheepish look in Jocelyn's direction.

She waited until they had gone into their bedroom, and then lifted Bernie on to her shoulder and carried him up to Phil.

12

Bill met up with his crew in the heliport at Aberdeen airport. As he crossed the lounge towards their usual table at the far side, he called a greeting here and there, but the responses were mostly just a raised arm or a movement of the head. Those who were happy to be back were in the minority. Most had left wives behind to look after the family and had the usual worries and longings that come from forced separation. The two weeks' off was behind them and an unremitting stint of long shifts was ahead.

There was a gloomy silence amongst those of his eight-man crew who had arrived before him, although Dugal, their driller, was scribbling away; he was two years into an Open University degree. The others sprawled in the grey, rounded seats or walked restlessly about, waiting for the call to put on their life gear and trek out to their helicopter for the flight to their oil rig, far out in the North Sea.

"What do you think of this, Bill?" Sweyn Jimson asked him, when he came across and dropped his rucksack. Sweyn held up a hand-held phone. "See, it fits in my pocket snugly and I can dial up anyone I want whenever I feel like it." Sweyn and he were the two roughnecks in their crew, working the drill pipes.

"Now, that is something I wouldn't mind having," Bill responded, reaching out for it as he sat down. Sweyn was a gadget freak. He had brought back a tiny television set after one shore leave (which only produced static) and a neat tape recorder after another, but it was frequently useless toys that he introduced into their shared bunk-room. The sort of things that scooted across the floor or climbed up walls making outlandish noises. Fortunately he soon tired of these and swapped them on.

"Who would you like to ring?"

"No one."

"Come on. What about Jo?"

Bill gave the phone back. "She's still away on holiday."

"Some holiday." Sweyn fiddled away with the digits on his phone, his eyes averted. Bill could feel his scepticism but he was not willing to admit to his abandonment.

They sat in silence watching a helicopter land and the blades slowly lose their impetus. The door was swung back and the passengers jumped down. The next flight was announced but it was still not theirs.

"Two to go yet," Sweyn said, looking up at the screen.

"At least there's no delay." Fog or gale force winds would have kept them hanging about. It was bad enough at that end but frustrating at the other, where the crews were waiting for the change over. "A coffee and sandwich?" he asked.

"I'm o.k."

Bill zigzagged between the tables to the food counter, turning to survey the crowd as he waited to be served. He didn't know many of the people who were lounging about. There were upwards of two hundred drilling rigs in the North Sea – drill-ships that worked deep water, semi-submersibles and jack-ups. The helicopter that he was waiting for had only room for his crew and their relief crew, but the helicopters came and went from their rig every few hours, with the change over of ancillary staff There were a lot of them. One journalist had described the rigs as industrial islands moving on the water. Bill smiled to himself as he thought of that. Sweyn lived on an island and had said that island life was nothing like life on a rig.

"What are you having?"

Bill was jogged out of his reverie and gave his order, returning to Sweyn with his tray.

"So, what is your island like?" he asked

Sweyn looked up from the technical magazine in which he was absorbed, his eyes a blur of incomprehension. "What brought that on?" he asked.

"I was just thinking about it. At least I was thinking about what that journalist said."

"He was a city waller," Sweyn responded dismissively, closing his magazine. "The first thing that hits me when I get home is the silence. Most days you can only hear the waves breaking on the shore below the house, or the animals bellowing in the byre, letting their needs be known."

"All right, cut the crap. What do you do up there?"

"Not much."

"Aren't you bored?"

"No."

"Well, what do you do?"

"I help my Dad a bit on the farm, go fishing or shooting, pass the time of day with anyone I come across, and meet up with my mates in the pub at night."

"What do you talk about?"

Sweyn laughed. "There's no lack of talk. Everyone knows everyone else's business and if they don't know it, they make it up."

"Charming. How many people are there?"

"About two hundred."

Bill whistled. "Do you know them all?"

"Probably."

"The weather will be freezing though."

"Not really. The gulf stream passes that way."

"I've heard that one before."

"But it's true. The weather is mild. Come up and see for yourself."

"Is that an invitation?"

"If you like."

"I might take you up on it."

"Come next time."

"I might do that. Just for the weekend though," he added, wondering if he had been too hasty in accepting the invitation. The place sounded a bit dull.

"I think there's going to be a ceilidh that Saturday."

When their flight was called, Bill gulped down the last of his coffee and threw his cigarette packet and matches onto the table. Nothing like that was allowed on the rig; he had to content himself with chewing gum. Sweyn was already heading for the gents and he followed him.

They had a two hour journey ahead, packed into survival suits.

13

Jocelyn looked down on the slab-roofed house. It was long and narrow, built snugly into the hillside facing the Atlantic Ocean.

"What a marvellous view!" she exclaimed, looking back at Thorfinn over her shoulder. They were walking in single-file along the heather-fringed path, high above Selkie Bay with the sea rippling in the breeze and the waves lapping against outlying rocks or spurting into crevices in the surrounding cliffs. "Your house is not so small."

"I only own half of it."

"Who lives in the other half?"

"An elderly couple. He's the groundsman at Trowsay House and his wife was the cook there when it was privately owned. She keeps an eye on the place for me, airing it and that sort of thing. We'll call in and see her."

Jocelyn turned round and said anxiously: "Hanna may wonder where we've got to if we're away too long."

"It's o.k. Hanna knows that we can't pass Mrs. McFea's door without calling in, and we can't call in without sitting down and passing the time of day."

"I feel a bit guilty about leaving her to finish painting the kitchen."

"Don't be. She's glad to get me out from under her feet."

Jocelyn smiled to herself, knowing that that was true. Hanna was a perfectionist and had sent Thorfinn off on different errands during the morning to keep him from wielding a paint brush with carefree abandon.

The path widened, and wended down to the two adjoined cottages. There was a peat stack in an open-fronted shed attached to the gable end, and Jocelyn could see a dusty, brown mark near the gutter where the peats had reached when they had been carted down from the hill the previous autumn; now there was only a ragged pile left at the bottom.

Thorfinn handed her down from the slope to a flagged close that ran the length of the building. He stopped at the first door and started to give a rat-a-tat-tat, but the door was opened before he had finished the rhythm.

"There you are then, Thorfinn," the elderly woman said. She was stout with smooth, downy cheeks and a number of chins that stretched and contracted with the movement of her head. Her thick-lensed spectacles had slipped down her nose, revealing heavy brown eyes, veined with age. "I was wondering when you were going to come across and see me."

"I came this way a few days ago but you weren't in."

"Aye, well, that may be so," she said, not giving in. Her absence from home could be explained by her recently set silver hair, waved and teased into loose curls. "But I expected you round as soon as you got back from your travels, to tell me all about it."

"I did come," Thorfinn replied with indignation, but she was not going to concede the point.

"And this is….."

"Jocelyn Fenwick," Thorfinn said, putting his hand on Jocelyn's back as he introduced her.

"I've heard all about you," Mrs. McFea said pleasantly.

She held on to Jocelyn's hand, scrutinising her closely. Jocelyn could see herself reflected and distorted in the thick lenses and smiled, wondering what she had heard. "Come away in."

"I'll just show Jocelyn my place first," Thorfinn told her.

Mrs. McFea straightened her shoulders, crossed her forearms beneath her ample bosom and regarded Thorfinn with a basilisk eye.

Thorfinn knew exactly what she was thinking and couldn't resist the temptation to play along. "Is it all aired and ready?" he asked.

"You can go next door, Thorfinn, but Mrs. Fenwick will stay here with me."

"That would hardly serve the purpose."

"You ought to be ashamed of yourself, Thorfinn."

"I'm sorry," Jocelyn intervened, bewildered at the turn the conversation had taken. "Thorfinn wants to show me his house."

"I've no doubt that he does."

Thorfinn relented: "I'm a reformed character, Mrs McFea," he assured her with a chuckle, putting his arms around her shoulders and giving her a hug. "My philandering days are over."

"I'm glad to hear it."

"Jocelyn is thinking of staying on and may want to rent my house. That's why we're here."

Mrs. McFea relaxed her rigid stance and brightened up. "It's a nice enough place for a single lady as you'll see for yourself," she said with an apologetic smile in Jocelyn's direction. "You'll come in by when you've finished looking round, won't you? I saw you coming and have got the kettle on."

Thorfinn's door was on the latch. It was always on the latch; there was no lock. When Jocelyn voiced her concern, Thorfinn whispered: "I'm afraid it is something that you'd have to live with. Mrs. McFea would be cut to the quick if you had a lock put on. She guards the place like a spider in her web."

"But she isn't here all the time."

"She would still see it as a slight on her integrity."

Thorfinn did the talking as he showed Jocelyn round. Her silence masked her horror at the place. It was clean and tidy (no doubt Mrs. McFea had seen to that) but it was a bachelor's pad indeed, and a bachelor who took little notice of his surroundings. The main room was a reasonable size, but the gas cooker was aged, the kitchen cupboards made of painted plywood and the furniture minimal; the carpet was not only faded but threadbare. The bathroom was on the left of the short passage leading through to the small bedroom and the only nod to modern living in the whole place was a shower installed above the claw-footed bath.

"It probably needs a bit done to it," Thorfinn said modestly as they worked their way back to the living room.

Jocelyn did not respond to this understatement, going over to look out of the window instead. The house had been built right on the cliff edge and the view out to sea was spectacular. Wispy bits of grass clung to the wall below the window ledge and she could see patches of pale purple thrift growing here and there on the surface of the cliffs that curved round to her right; there was a multitude of sea birds either flying or perched on insubstantial ledges, their cries partly muffled by the thickness of the walls. Thorfinn came across and stood beside her, identifying the different birds at her request.

"You could do the place up in lieu of rent," Thorfinn ventured, sensing that her dismay at the cottage's stark and shabby condition had been mitigated by its position.

"I think I would need to do quite a bit of work before moving in."

"So you will take it?"

"I've not decided to come back to Trowsay yet."

"Hanna and I would be just over the hill at the farmhouse and Mrs. McFea is discreet. You could spend nights on the other side of the island without her blabbing."

"Now, why would I want to do that?"

Thorfinn chuckled, putting his arm across her shoulders as they turned towards the door. "You tell me."

Jocelyn smiled, walking out of his arm without answering.

In contrast to Thorfinn's end of the building, the McFea living room was stuffed with furniture. There were colourful ornaments and knick-knacks displayed on the walls, the ledge above the old fashioned black range with its oven attached, and on every shelf of the antique dresser. The table was set and the smell of baking scones mingled with the fragrance of burning peat.

"We can't stay too long," Thorfinn said, realising that the baking scones were going to form part of a substantial meal that Mrs. McFea had rustled up in the short time that they had been next door. "We left Hanna painting over at Selkie and she'll be a bit miffed to hear that we have been feasting while she has been slaving."

"I'll give her a ring and ask her to come over."

"You can't. I'm afraid that an over-zealous Pete Gunn severed the phone cable this morning."

"Ah well then, there's nothing to be done. Sit yourselves down and tell me what has been going on over there. A skeleton found in the barn! Whatever next!"

"You probably know as much as we do."

"Callum is not a great talker," she said, introducing her husband into the conversation. She sat down in her rocker and directed them to the two-seater sofa, with a wave of her hand. "Did you know that I lived there when I was a child, Thorfinn?"

"Yes, I knew that. Were you a relation of the Maconachies?"

"I'm glad to say that I was not," was the forceful response. "Auntie Maconachie was a fearsome woman who got pleasure out of chastisement, under the direction of her bible. No, I was fostered out." Thorfinn raised his eyebrow in query and she continued: "My folks worked at Trowsay House and they couldn't keep me there with them."

"That's awful!" Jocelyn exclaimed.

"Aye, well, that was the way of it then." She leaned over and hitched open the side-oven . "My Mum was the cook and Dad the head gardener. No doubt I wasn't expected because my Mum was in her mid-forties when I was born." A finger gently pressed on the top of the nearest scone gave her the answer she wanted. "They're ready now. Once I've got this tray out, I'll get the tea on the go."

"Let me help you," Thorfinn offered, getting up and going round the back of her chair.

"Fine that." She took off her oven glove and handed it to him, before pushing herself up with the help of the armrests. "But don't drop them mind."

"I wouldn't dare."

When they were settled at the table with fragile, porcelain cups of strong tea and hot scones dripping with butter, Mrs. McFea said: "I hear they've finished in the barn. Did they give up looking for more bodies?"

"They dug a bit round where the skeleton lay but that was all."

"I thought they'd be lifting the whole floor to see what they could find."

"Hanna was hoping for that. It would have saved her a bit of money if the police had removed all the cobbles and concrete for her."

"She'll have the money to do it now though," Mrs. McFea ventured, eying Thorfinn thoughtfully as he mopped some butter off his chin with the linen napkin provided. "You've done well for yourself, Thorfinn."

He responded placidly: "I always wanted to be a kept man."

"I don't know about that, but you're not the layabout that you once were," Mrs. McFea conceded.

"The compliment is accepted with gratitude."

"But she's getting her side of the bargain too."

"I'll tell Hanna what you said, if she becomes uppity."

"Get on with you." If she had been sitting nearer to him, Mrs. McFea's elbow would have dug him in the ribs. "So tell me now, why are they not looking for more bodies if it's an ancient burial site?"

"It's not. They're now sure that there was only the one body and it was put there reasonably recently."

Mrs. McFea was literally knocked back in her chair by that disclosure

"How could that be? "she asked in astonishment.

Jocelyn told her about the new concrete.

"But that means nothing. I remember work being done in the barn."

"They also found a piece of fabric that had not disintegrated."

Mrs. McFea did not seem to take that in because she went on: "I remember that time because Alec got the hiding of his life. We were told not to go into the barn but of course, as soon as Alec thought the coast was clear, he was opening the door a slit and looking in."

"What did he see?" Jocelyn asked eagerly.

"Nothing." Mrs. McFea held her tea cup in her hand for a moment and took a sip before laying it back on the saucer. "Not anything that sticks in my mind anyway."

"So the farmer could have been burying a body."

Mrs. McFea's chins wobbled in amusement. "You're letting your imagination run away with you, my dear. There was no body. Uncle Maconachie would be reconcreting one of the stalls while the cattle were out for the summer. Auntie wouldn't want us trailing dirt into the house, that's all."

"But you said that Alec was.....physically abused."

"He was thrashed for disobedience," Mrs. McFea said, leaning over and refilling the cups. "It was always happening and, no doubt, that time she was in a particularly bad mood."

"Poor boy."

"You're right on that score."

The conversation reverted to other topics and when

they had finished making a dent in all that was put in front of them, it was time for them to leave.

"I wouldn't mind seeing what you're up to over there," Mrs. McFea said at the door. "I know about the extension but I hear you've knocked down the walls separating the living room from the bedrooms."

Thorfinn gave her a rundown of the changes they had made and agreed to come the next day with the Range Rover to take her across.

As they started back up the coastal path, Jocelyn asked him what the road was like between there and the cave.

"Not too bad. It is under-used and is covered with weeds but it has a solid foundation."

"It can't be easy driving though and such a long way round."

"I suppose so; but Mrs. McFea can't manage this walk over the hill, and I don't mind going for her. In fact I will enjoy it."

Jocelyn knew that that was true.

"It is not just that it will give me a good excuse to avoid the chores for the duration," he said wryly, correctly interpreting her silence; "parts of that coast are the most picturesque on the island. The track meanders round the various bays and you can scramble down to some intriguing isolated beaches. You should explore it some time."

"I will."

"A number of them provide seclusion for the grey seals during the pupping season."

"When is that?"

"In the autumn."

They conversed amicably as they made their way back.

Thorfinn pointed out unusual features in the geological structure of the cliffs and stopped now and then to crouch down and touch the different mosses and tiny plants growing near the cliff edge, giving them names. Jocelyn found this close-up inspection fascinating; before that, she had seen the mass of vegetation near the cliff tops as either tightly-packed coloured mosses or assorted grasses and not as a carpet of individual plants. She knew that Thorfinn was a naturalist and had a degree in biophysics but he carried his learning lightly and was unpretentious in imparting knowledge. It was an eye-opener for her to see that side of his character and she told him so.

Thorfinn smiled softly as he put out his hand to help her up. "And you, Jocelyn? Have you got another side to your character?"

She walked on for a bit in front of him before speaking: "Most people hide, or try to hide, the less acceptable parts of their personality. It is only small children who are open and truly natural."

"True."

They rounded the bay and were starting up towards the house, when Hanna climbed out of a front window with a haversack on her back.

She waved and called out when they were within hearing distance: "Come on; let's go down to the beach for lunch. I need a break." She linked arms with them both, smiling at Jocelyn and asking her about her botany lesson. "I was watching you being lectured," she went on with amusement and Jocelyn responded in the same light manner, while Thorfinn changed his position so that he had a woman on each arm.

"That's better," he said, smiling down at them, one at

a time, and Jocelyn felt a wave of pure happiness at being accepted into their close circle.

14

The clanging of a school bell being swung in the hall reverberated up through the well of the house. Heads popped over banisters to hear what Phil had to say.

"Telephone for you, Jocelyn," Phil called up. Atlanticscape was a large house and there were only three telephones. The main line was on the table in the hall with an extension on the first landing and another in Phil's workshop. This clanging alert saved Phil's legs when there was either a phone call or a need to contact someone in the house.

"Who is it?" Jocelyn called down, but Phil had turned back into the kitchen and did not reply. She began to walk slowly down the stairs to the extension on the landing below, collecting her thoughts. She had not left her number when she telephoned Bill and had not thought that he would be able to trace her call.

"Hallo," she said quietly, waiting for an outburst of condemnation and girning self-pity, but it was Rab Ballater at the other end of the phone; she relaxed in relief.

"How have you been?" Rab asked. "I saw you passing yesterday and waved but you took no notice."

"I smiled."

"I missed that smile."

"Hanna and Thorfinn waved," she said, opening the spare bedroom door and sitting down on the bed. "I thought I would be discreet."

"Your discretion is wasted. Everyone knows already that you and I are sweethearts."

"Everyone except us."

"But that can soon be rectified."

"You go too fast, Rab. Despite the talk, we are still virtual strangers."

There was a pause before he said quietly: "I don't feel that we are."

"How was your trip home?"

"This is my home."

"You know what I mean."

"I know that you skilfully changed the subject."

"You were trying to trap me."

"Quite right."

She laughed. "Why did you telephone?"

"I didn't telephone. Phil rang me."

"Really!

"Yes, really."

"Why?"

"He has invited me to dinner tomorrow night so that we can all go down to the ceilidh together."

"I would like that," Jocelyn said quietly. They had been talking about the ceilidh while they painted at the farmhouse and she had voiced her regret at missing it. Hanna had said that Rab would probably bring her along after their meal but it would be nicer to meet everyone as a group rather than as a couple.

"I wanted to have you to myself."

"There are other evenings."

"What about tonight?"

Jocelyn immediately thought of her hair which needed a wash.

"Just come as you are," Rab said, sensing that a refusal was in the offing. "I haven't washed my hair either."

Jocelyn giggled. "How did you know that that was what I was thinking?"

"My experience of the female sex."

Jocelyn was about to make a frivolous remark but she stopped herself; it would have been inappropriate in his circumstance. "All right. I'll come over in about an hour or so."

"My heart is already starting to throb in anticipation."

"You are offering to take me out for a meal, aren't you? Nothing more."

"Naturally."

Jocelyn could hear him chuckling as they finished the call, which left her wondering about his intentions.

She was right to wonder.

Rab came out of the house to greet her and when they reached his door, he swept her up and carried her over the threshold. She slipped down in his arms, fitting into the curves of his body, her knees trembling and her stomach plummeting with desire. He kissed her hair, her forehead and down the length of her nose before touching the rounded bow of her lips gently. The effect was magnetic.

"You have a delicious mouth," Rab whispered, taking her hand and guiding her upstairs to a back room where the bed was turned down and the electric fire glowed.

"This is obviously a pre-meditated seduction," Jocelyn said, with a shivering laugh and lowered eyelids, as he started to undo the buttons of her blouse.

"I was a boy scout in my youth and I have always believed in the motto: "Be prepared," he murmured as he started kissing the parts of her flesh which gradually became exposed.

Jocelyn dropped her skirt, saying breathlessly: "The boy scouts and the girl guides."

He responded to her dictates until all self-control evaporated and their mutual passion took hold.

After descending from the heavens and luxuriating in a slow parting of their bodies, Rab fell asleep. Jocelyn did not mind. She knew that he would have had a physically exhausting day on the farm and it was natural that he would flake out when totally relaxed. He was a big man and they were cramped together in the small bed. She could feel the warmth and sweet smell of his exhaling breath on her shoulder and the weight of his arm across her breasts. The desire to move became overwhelming and she gently lifted his arm. He opened his eyes and smiled at her before moving nearer the wall and putting his arm loosely around her shoulders instead.

"That was lovely," he said, shutting his eyes briefly before exhaling his breath in a long sigh of contentment. "I knew as soon as I saw you that you were my sort of girl."

"And what sort is that?" Jocelyn asked teasingly, moving closer.

"A beautiful girl without inhibitions."

"You are wrong, Rab. I am generally very strait-laced."

"Even better. A beautiful, strait-laced girl without inhibitions." He turned towards her, his intentions clear, but she slipped out of bed.

"I must go to the bathroom."

"Me too. Start running the bath while you're there. I'll go downstairs."

Jocelyn had not shared a bath since she was a child and it was a novel experience to share it with a large man. Rab took the tap end, making a pillow out of towels so that he could lie back, and there was much splashing and laughter as toes found tickly and erotic places. They had two plunges in the bath because once out the first time, the inevitable happened.

"I'm hungry," Jocelyn admitted when they were drying themselves with two large bath towels.

"Me too."

"Are we going out?"

"Do you want to?"

"Have you got anything to eat here?"

"Lots."

They wrapped themselves in their towels and went back to the back bedroom.

"We'd better dress," Rab said. "Who knows? We might get visitors."

"Do you think so?" Jocelyn asked in horror, immediately aware of her compromising situation.

Rob chuckled. "No, I don't think so. I just wanted to see your reaction to the possibility."

Rab wanted to dress her. She had had men undress her in the past but dressing her was a new experience which caused a lot of fondling and much laughter, as he tried to pack her into her bra and fasten it at the back.

"Let me do it," she said after his second attempt, but he said that he was never defeated by a problem, even of that magnitude.

Once they were downstairs, Rab dropped the blind on the kitchen window and turned on the fan heater, while Jocelyn opened his fridge to see what could be made. She expected to find easy cook ingredients, like eggs and cheese, and was amazed to see every shelf stacked with home-cooked meals.

"You certainly won't starve," she commented.

"When it comes to food," he said, stroking her silky black hair as she crouched to inspect the different meals on offer. "I seem to have become a member of everyone's family. As soon as it was known that I was back, food started arriving."

"Can't you cook?"

"I pride myself on my cooking," he responded with mock outrage, "although I have to admit my repertoire is small."

"Out of the frying pan into the mouth."

"Something like that," he smiled.

They had chicken broth that one of the farmer's wives had delivered earlier in the day, an omelette with cold roast beef on the side and delicious apple and raisin tart with ice cream. Conversation between them was easy as they related their very different experiences of life. They had opposing views on government intervention and political solutions to economic problems but their arguments were mild and light-hearted.

While Rab was putting on the kettle for coffee, Jocelyn said: "I saw Thorfinn's cottage a few days ago."

Rab turned to her with a startled expression; Jocelyn knew what he was thinking.

"He didn't lure me into his den for immoral purposes," she assured him, adding mischievously, "like one man I know."

"That must be a first," Rab said, his face creasing in a smile. "You have to keep two eyes on randy Thorfinn."

"He's honourable in his way."

"I bet." Rab poured two coffees and brought them to the table. "So, why were you visiting his cottage?"

Jocelyn explained about losing the urge to spend all her time painting and not wanting to pray on Phil's hospitality. Rab opened his mouth to speak, but she held up her hand: "I must go back home to sort things out," she said seriously, "but I like it here and I want to come back. Thorfinn suggested that I rent or even buy his pad, as he called it."

Rab twiddled with his spoon. "I can't see you there."

"It is rather awful isn't it?"

"Hanna hated it."

"But if it was done up, it could make a reasonable holiday home."

"Is it just a holiday home that you want"

"I'm not really thinking about anything clearly at the moment."

Rab reached for her hand. "I would be sorry to see you go."

The sincerity of his words and the comforting strength of his fingers overwhelmed her with a love that she had never felt in that intensity before – at least not for a grown man.

"Me, too," she whispered unsteadily, her eyes filling with tears.

"Jocelyn, darling, what is it?"

"Don't take any notice," she gulped, pulling a handkerchief from her pocket. "I sometimes get over-emotional, that's all."

"Come here." He took her on his knee and held her close. "What's the matter?"

His strength and compassion were too much for her to bear, and the dam that had held her memories in check, disintegrated, everything flooding out.

"Shush now." Rab said softly when she had finished, stroking her hair away from her face and kissing her eyelids. "We cannot change the past, but everything will work out all right for you now, you'll see."

She put her arms around his neck, resting her cheek against his shoulder and wept. He let her cry, stroking her hair tenderly and murmuring words of comfort until her sorrow for the wasted years of regret and guilt were spent.

"Feeling better?" Rab asked, gently wiping the tears from her cheeks with his fingers.

Jocelyn gave a nod and a half smile.

"Come on then," he said, lifting her from his knee. He held her against him for a moment, before kissing her briefly on the lips. "Let's see if I can find a video to cheer you up."

15

It was past midnight before Jocelyn got back to Atlanticscape and the morning was well advanced before she began to surface, holding on to and luxuriating in warm half-dreams, while knowing, deep down, that it was time to get up. Eventually she lifted reluctant eyelids to check the time on her bedside clock, and was awake instantly. It was ten minutes to ten. There was a cold mug of tea beside the clock, which meant that Phil had come in without her hearing him, and left this token of his affection. He had brought her tea before when she had overslept, but this time he had not woken her.

Once she was showered and dressed, she went up to his workshop, walking into a companionable silence. Phil was concentrating on gently chiselling a piece of wood with a narrow file and Bernie was asleep on the chair at the window.

"Wait a sec," Phil cautioned and went on filing the intricate top of a rock stack, while Bernie fell off his chair, rolled over and righted himself to give her his exuberant welcome. Phil was totally absorbed, unaware of the movement around him. "That's it, I think," he said, stepping back from his bench and ducking to look down and through a roughly hewed arch at the front. This was his first rock stack, although it was still mostly attached to the solid block of uncarved wood.

"You've got on well," Jocelyn said, turning her attention from the demanding dog to Phil's creation.

"It's a bit ticklish at the moment."

"I bet it is. One slip of the knife or the chisel and the whole thing is ruined."

Phil smiled down at her and wished her a good morning. "It's not as bad as that," he went on, after they had exchanged greetings, "at the worst, it would mean altering the original idea a bit." He gave a toneless whistle through his teeth as he fitted the lantern into its rounded space at the side and turned it on. The outer glass slowly turned and the light flickered against the carving, casting moving shadows. "That's one hurdle overcome," he said with satisfaction, "but I'll not know if the light creates plausible dancing shadows until I've nearly finished the rough hewing."

"It's already very impressive."

Phil brushed the file he had been using and hung it up. "I heard you coming in last night," he said.

"Did I waken you?"

"I wanted to be sure that you got back safely."

"What if I had stayed over?" Jocelyn asked mischievously.

"I hadn't thought about that."

"Neither had I."

Phil looked at her anxiously. "But you like him."

"Very much."

"Good, because I have asked him for dinner."

"I know. Can I help you get it ready?"

"It's all done."

Jocelyn went up on tiptoes to kiss him on the cheek. "You're a lovely, thoughtful man, Phil. It will be easier for me to meet prying eyes with your support."

He flushed with pleasurable embarrassment. "What are you going to be up to today?" he asked, touching her cheek lightly.

"I'll give Hanna a hand. She's starting to rub down the floorboards in the enlarged sittingroom. It will be a tedious job. There are different stains painted round the skirting in all three of the original rooms."

"I haven't been across for a long time," he said regretfully, "but I'm sure it's all in hand. Hanna is very efficient." Bernie was still hanging around his feet and he scooped him up and carried him back to his chair. "By the way, you may find a visitor there and little work being done. Thorfinn's former neighbour wanted to see the place and they were picking her up."

"I know that. I met Mrs. McFea yesterday," Jocelyn told him, sauntering across to join him in the window alcove. "In fact, she invited us in for a lavish morning cuppa."

Phil raised his eyebrows in query.

"Thorfinn was showing me his cottage."

"I hope you're not thinking of moving there."

"Not right away. That is, if you can put up with me for a bit longer."

Phil said that she was welcome to stay as long as she wanted.

"That's kind, but I can't stay here for ever."

"I wouldn't object."

Jocelyn murmured thanks, adding with quiet seriousness: "But you know that is not going to happen, Phil." She lent against the shutter and started fiddling with a button on her blouse. "Your offer of a painting break was a godsend for me at the time, and the complete change has made me see things more clearly, but I am used to having my own place."

"I can understand." Phil bent to stroke Bernie's head

and allowed his hand to be grasped lightly and played with; like a baby, the puppy was still exploring things with his mouth. "It's strange the way things work out, isn't it," he went on thoughtfully, "having you all here has been a transition period for me too. The house was empty after Duncan passed on and it is far too big for me on my own, but I didn't want to leave. My memories of him and our life together were still too raw." He looked out of the window with a dejected stoop to his shoulders and then turned back, giving a sweeping gesture that embraced his surroundings, before dropping his hand. "But when Hanna goes, I think I will sell up and move on."

"Where would you go?"

"I'll see what turns up, but I won't leave Trowsay for good."

"It does have a special magic."

"Not so much magic as a feeling of belonging somewhere in the world; having a place in people's memories; a place where you are not alone."

"You would miss it."

"I would."

"And be missed," she said softly, taking his arm and sharing with him the view over the rugged moorland to the slate-grey sea in the distance. The clouds parted briefly, and a beam of sunlight passed quickly over, giving colour and movement to the sea, and brightness to the muted greens and rusts of the land. "How long have you lived here?"

"About ten years." He leaned forward to clear a smudge on the window with the sleeve of his aged, misshapen sweater. "This was my first proper home. I think I told you that we met when Duncan asked me to make a frame for one of his large paintings. He was very fussy about the colour and style, calling round to my workshop nearly every day to see how the work was progressing." He paused, a memory softening his eyes and lifting the folds in his face. "He changed my life."

"I'm sure you changed his too."

"Perhaps." He glanced down at her with gentle affection, patting the hand on his arm before detaching himself. "Off you go now, Jocelyn, and let me get on. The morning is nearly over and little done."

When Jocelyn reached the farmhouse, she found Hanna on her knees with a scraper in her hand. It held a noxious brown accumulation of moistened paint and the acrid smell of nitromorse was heavy in the air. There was no sign of Thorfinn.

"Sorry to be so late," Jocelyn said, her voice echoing round the empty room. "Just let me change and I'll be with you in a minute."

"Would you open a window first? I can't stand much more of this."

Jocelyn went across and swung open one of the newly fitted windows, taking the opportunity to breathe in a lungful of cool, clear air.

"That's better," Hanna said, wiping the gunge from her scraper on to a piece of newspaper and disposing of it in a cardboard box beside her.

Jocelyn's painting clothes were on the floor in the kitchen and she came back into the room wearing paint-stained jeans and an old shirt over her sweater. "Where's Thorfinn?" she asked, lifting the tin of nitromorse from the makeshift table.

"He's taken Mrs. McFea to the police station," Hanna told her, rocking back on her heels and watching Jocelyn pour the think substance into an open-topped plastic pot.

"Has she lost something?"

"No, nothing like that. The police rang her. Evidently they found some valuable things in the grave – jewellery, ornaments and such like – and they wanted her to call in and see if she could identify anything. They think they were stolen from Trowsay House back in the thirties."

"So he was a burglar?"

"Sounds like it."

"A bit extreme to kill the man, even if he was making off with the family silver."

"I don't suppose they meant to kill him."

Jocelyn picked up her filled container and a scraper, and took her place on the floor at the point where Hanna had started, so that she could work her way round to meet her. "Would the Maconachies have had much of value to steal?"

"The police seem pretty sure that the stuff came from Trowsay House."

Jocelyn thought about that for a bit while she painted a patch of stain. "Perhaps one of the Maconachies stole things from Trowsay House over the years and then the burglar tried to steal it from them," she suggested.

"That's a bit unlikely."

"There was a connection between the two places through Mrs. McFea. She was telling us about it yesterday."

"I know."

Jocelyn got up and went looking for some newspapers. Hanna offered a few from her pile and said that there were more in the utility room "Bring a cardboard box too," she called, "or a plastic bag."

When Jocelyn came back, carrying an old cardboard box and another lot of newspapers, she continued with the conversation where they had left off: "I would have thought that whoever struck the blow that killed him, would just have buried the body and kept mum about the burglary."

"Not if it took place at Trowsay House."

"Why?"

"The maids or the daily help would see evidence of a break-in and that could not be kept quiet here."

Jocelyn smiled. "But the death could."

"He probably came from the mainland."

"Ah, that dim and distant land," Jocelyn said with a laugh, settling back down on the floor. "The source of all ills."

"But probably true in this instance."

"It would certainly explain why some stolen goods were put in the grave with the body," Jocelyn mused, dipping her brush in the nitromorse and painting another area of floor with the dissolving gel. "Both the burglar and the loot disappeared together."

"Exactly."

"What was Mrs. McFea saying about it?"

"She was adamant that she would not be able to identify anything. She moved away from Trowsay at the start of the war when she was five and she was only in the front of the house when the owners were away on holiday."

They worked in silence for a bit, lifting the moistened paint from the area in front of them several times, wiping their scrapers on the old pieces of newspaper and then wriggling backwards to paint another stretch. There were layers of stain and each patch had to be done several times before the wood was brought back to its natural colour.

"Did you enjoy your evening?" Hanna asked, breaking into Jocelyn's thoughts.

"Yes thanks," Jocelyn said automatically. "It was great." The opening was there for her to introduce Rab into the conversation but she was still revelling in the glow and closeness of her new experience and wanted to keep her secret thoughts and flights of fancy to herself. She knew that Hanna would be discreet but once her experience was shared and talked over, it would lose its special intimacy. "How long have they been away?"

"Ages. They should be back soon."

They worked on until they heard the distant sound of the Range Rover slowing down and starting up the track. Their ears were attuned to its particular gear change.

"That's them," Hanna said, getting to her feet and rubbing her back. "And it's time for a break. Let's put the kettle on."

"I haven't done much yet."

"That doesn't matter. Aren't you eager to hear what they have to say?"

"Of course."

"Come on then. We can do this later."

They could hear Mrs. McFea's voice berating Thorfinn before they appeared. The method he had used to get her down from the high front seat seemed to be the trouble.

"I'm not a bag of tatties," she was saying as they crossed

the courtyard towards the open door in the extension. "You should have more respect for my person."

"I thought you'd like to be swung down. Make you feel young again."

"To lose my dignity and fall into your arms, like a hussy?"

The idea of Mrs. McFea being a hussy made the girls giggle.

"You were certainly a delicious armful."

"Stop it now, Thorfinn. I know you're having fun at my expense and I won't have it." They came through the door, Mrs. McFea leaning on Thorfinn's arm. "You should keep your man in order, Hanna. I'm grateful for the trouble he's taken but he's right aggravating."

Hanna agreed that he was, directing her to one of the two old armchairs that sat incongruously in the middle of the new modern kitchen. Mrs. McFea swept her hand over the seat of the one she chose, before easing herself down.

"I'm right glad to have that over," she said, giving a sigh as she relaxed against the upholstery. "It's not an experience I would want to repeat."

"A cup of tea," Hanna offered, pulling the flex out of the bubbling kettle.

"Make it good and strong now," Mrs. McFea instructed, and watched balefully as Hanna dropped a teabag into a common mug. Hanna added another tea bag, and gave it a robust stir before extracting the offending squares.

"Now, tell us all about it," Hanna encouraged, holding the milk carton over the noxious brew and offering milk and sugar. "Was it a man or a woman's skeleton?"

"We didn't ask that, did we Thorfinn?"

"I assume it was a man."

"Aye, more than likely."

"Were you able to identify anything?" Jocelyn asked.

Mrs. McFea did not immediately reply. She accepted a splash of milk and swallowed a mouthful of tea with a shudder before saying: "I was."

"Would you like a biscuit?" Hanna offered, fiddling with the top of a packet of digestives.

"I'm too upset to be eating anything," Mrs. McFea declared, handing Thorfinn her mug to put on the draining board beside him. He had a grin on his face, knowing that Mrs. McFea liked her tea made in a proper teapot and poured over milk, into a china cup.

"What happened?" Hanna asked, giving up her attempt to prise open the top of the packet with a knife.

Mrs. McFea did not reply. She just opened her handbag and lifted out a tissue, loosely wrapped round a small item. From this, she took a ring, holding it in the palm of her hand for everyone to see. At its centre was a blue cameo surrounded by tiny pearls.

"Is it yours?" Jocelyn asked mystified.

Mrs. McFea swallowed once or twice and dabbed at her eyes with the tissue, overcome with emotion.

"It was her mother's ring," Thorfinn told them. He was relaxing against the sink, his ankles crossed and his arms folded.

"The only jewellery my Mum had was a marquisate broach and her wedding band. I only saw this ring once, but she spoke about it often. It was left to her by her grandmother and it was a prized possession." She paused; no one spoke, waiting for her to recover her voice. "And they found it out there in the mud, all jumbled together with the other things. The folks over there at Trowsay House could afford the loss, and no doubt claimed for it on their insurance, but it was criminal to take my Mum's ring."

Hanna and Jocelyn agreed and the ring was passed over for them to inspect and praise before being handed back.

"Was there any problem about claiming it?" Hanna asked.

"There was. That's what took the time."

"Mrs. McFea is a very determined woman,"Thorfinn remarked, his face creasing in amused reminiscence.

She ignored his interruption. "The sergeant was a stranger to these parts and he didn't believe it was my Mum's ring. He wanted me to show evidence of ownership, and blethered on about corroboration from other parties, insurance and such like things. I ask you!" Remembering the insult to her integrity, rekindled Mrs. McFea's outrage. "Folks like my parents didn't have insurance."

"So what happened?" Hanna asked.

It was Thorfinn who replied: "To begin with, the conversation went round in circles. The sergeant wouldn't release the ring and Mrs. McFea wouldn't leave without it. There seemed to be an impasse until I remembered Willie Kylison."

"I should have remembered him myself."

"Who is Willie Kylison?" Jocelyn asked

"A retired policeman who lives on his family farm just along the coast from here,"Thorfinn told her.

"He wasn't just a policeman," Mrs. McFea corrected him. "Willie was an important man in the police force down south."

"The main thing is that he gave you a good character reference…."

"And why wouldn't he? I've known him since he was a lad."

"It did the trick anyway."

"Aye, it did."

"And the find of your ring proved that everything came from Trowsay House," Hanna said.

"I suppose it did."

"Could you identify anything else?"

"I could not," Mrs. McFea said, dismissing the other stolen items with a shrug. "They held no interest for me."

Thorfinn enlightened them by listing the items he remembered.

"All stolen, for no purpose."

"There must have been a reason for putting the stuff in the grave," Hanna said, opening the fridge and looking at its contents thoughtfully, before taking out a bowl of soup and the ingredients to make sandwiches. "Jocelyn and I have been discussing it and we think that he was buried with the valuables so that everyone would believe that he had managed to get away."

"And if he was caught red-handed at Trowsay House," Jocelyn added, putting in her pennyworth, "he could have been struck a blow which killed him."

"But how did he come to be buried in the barn here?" Thorfinn asked.

"That's a bit of a mystery," Jocelyn admitted

"How well did your parents know the Maconachies, Mrs. McFea?"

"Well, enough," Mrs. McFea replied with a grimace.

She had been concentrating on her ring, trying to fit it on each finger in turn, and had only been half listening to the exchanges going on around her, but she suddenly got the drift of the conversation and asked sharply: "What has that to do with anything? Are you suggesting that my Dad killed this fellow and then got the Maconachies to bury the body?"

Hanna was taken aback by the vehemence of her reply and was shocked into silence.

Thorfinn came to her rescue: "She was not suggesting that it was him. It could have been the old man or someone else living in the house."

"My Dad was a law abiding man, I can tell you, and if he had apprehended a burglar and struck him down, he would have taken the consequences."

"Accidents can happen to anyone...."Thorfinn began, but he was interrupted by an irate Mrs. McFea.

"It is no accident to bury a fellow human being like a dog."

"I'm sorry," Hanna murmured.

"And you thought that the Maconachies would bury the body in their barn to help my Dad out. The very idea!"

"I thought they would be close friends with you staying here."

"They paid through the nose for that."

"Forgive me, Mrs. McFea. I did not mean to offend you."

"Ah, well, I suppose you didn't, but if you had known my Dad, or my Mum for that matter, you would not have thought such a thing."

The atmosphere in the kitchen was awkward. No

one spoke. The three of them just stood around, watching Mrs. McFea ease the ring off her little finger and start rewrapping it in the tear-stained tissue.

"There is nothing to show that he was killed while doing the burglary," Jocelyn blurted out, to lower the tension. "Someone else could have bumped him off and buried his body in the barn during the night, without the Maconachies knowing."

"That's not possible, Jocelyn. Concrete takes two or three days to dry."

"You mean the Maconachies must have been involved?"

"I fear so," Thorfinn went on. "They would've had to be away for several days at that particular time, not to notice anything."

"They never went away."

"Well, if they were here at the time, they must have known the burglar."

"That doesn't make any sense to me," Mrs. McFea stated. "They kept themselves very much to themselves. In fact, I can only remember a stranger here once, a big man who laughed a lot. He would play tricks on Auntie and she never told him off."

"He must've been a lover then," Thorfinn suggested naughtily, knowing that he would get a rise with that suggestion, and he was not disappointed. When Mrs. McFea had finished scoffing, Jocelyn suggested that he might have been a brother.

"Aye, he could have been. She had one brother, but I don't know if that was him or not." Mrs. McFea opened her handbag and laid the ring carefully back in, folding the tissue over. "Auntie didn't come from these parts, so any relation of hers would have travelled from over by."

"Highly suspicious," Thorfinn murmured laconically.

"I remember the stranger taking me on his knee and singing nursery rhymes," she said, smiling in reminiscence. "He tried to teach me cats' cradles too but the string was always getting snarled."

"How old were you?"

"Just a wee thing but I remember him because he was kind; different from the rest."

Thorfinn moved away from the sink so that Hanna could fill the kettle. "What do you think happened, Mrs. McFea?" he asked. "You were the only one here."

"And my memory isn't what it used to be. But one thing I will say, Auntie Maconachie was a terrifying woman but she was not a murderer. That would've been breaking a commandment."

"The sixth."

Thorfinn turned to Hanna in amazement. "How do you remember that?" he asked.

"It was drilled into me at school."

"In Norwegian?"

"Of course."

"What do the Norse say about stealing?"

"You don't need to be told."

"True. I wonder how the bigoted Mrs. Maconachie would react if she found that she was harbouring a thief?"

"She would not have countenanced it," Mrs. McFea said, with a grimace of memory 'Thou shalt not steal,' was a frequently quoted commandment in this house. If Alec and I didn't ask her first and took something to eat or play with, it was stealing."

"So she would be as mad as hell if she found her

brother in this house with stolen goods"

"But wouldn't she just have sent him packing," Jocelyn commented reasonably.

"Perhaps she intended to do that but things got out of hand. We know that she was a woman with a terrible temper."

"Wait a bit now," Mrs. McFea murmured, plumbing the depths of her memory. She had her handbag on her knee and was clutching the handle tightly with her gnarled fingers as she thought back to a distant time. "I remember waking one night and hearing Auntie's raised voice and sounds that made me think that she was beating Alec, but I could hear Alec breathing behind the screen that separated our beds. I fell asleep again quickly but I never thought that it was just a dream. I remember wondering the next morning if she had been beating Uncle Maconachie. That seemed possible to my childish mind but it was very unlikely. This was a silent house. They rarely spoke."

"So she could have vented her rage on her brother when she found out that he had done a burglary on her patch...."

"... and he fell back and hit his head on something ..."

"... and was killed instantly...."

"... which would explain why he was buried here with the loot."

Hanna and Jocelyn exchanged smiles as they made the story up together.

Thorfinn gave them a silent clap before turning to Mrs. McFea and asking if that episode had been just before they were doing work in the barn.

"When you're a bairn," she responded slowly, "you

remember events because they are different or special but you remember them in isolation, not in sequence."

"But it could've been?"

"I'm not saying it was and I'm not saying it wasn't. But the man buried in the barn isn't Auntie Maconachie's brother. He emigrated to Canada and got married out there. I can remember her reading that piece aloud from one of his letters. And, of course, he had a daughter."

"The letters could've been faked to throw everyone off the scent," Thorfinn pointed out.

"She would sit here, in this chair, reading bits out, with the airmail envelope lying on her lap. You know the kind, with red and blue bits round the edges."

"Available at any stationer."

"No doubt. But the letters seemed real enough."

Hanna reminded them that the daughter could not be traced.

"Perhaps she never existed," Thorfinn suggested.

"It is all too long ago to be certain about anything," Hanna said, reaching for a wooden spoon to stir the soup that she had set to heat. "You can't get much evidence from a skeleton."

"You could get DNA from it," Jocelyn pointed out, offering to help Hanna fill the rolls. "They could match that with the DNA from one of Alec's relatives. That would confirm if it was the brother, or rule him out."

"Alec's only close relative was his cousin in Canada," Mrs. McFea reminded them.

"And that's a non-starter."

"They could get it from something Alec used," Thorfinn suggested. "Combs, razors, pillows, that sort of thing. Have you thrown all the rubbish out, Hanna?"

"Everything except …" She stopped but she had looked across at the two armchairs and she did not need to finish her sentence. Mrs. McFea stiffened, the colour rising in her cheeks. "… but that's not likely."

"It's amazing what they can do nowadays," Thorfinn said insensitively.

Mrs. McFea moved forward in her seat, lifting her hand to her recently washed hair, "I doubt if either of these chairs has had a clean since Auntie passed on so they'll no doubt find the evidence they want," she said, leaning on the armrest. "I'll thank you to help me up, Thorfinn."

"I hoped you would stay for a sandwich lunch," Hanna said, indicating the soup pan and the rolls that she and Jocelyn were preparing.

"Another time. I've had a difficult morning and I'm not as young as I used to be." She took both ofThorfinn's hands, allowing herself to be pulled to her feet, her handbag swinging on her arm. She tottered a bit and straightened her green-flecked, tweed coat. "I haven't seen everything I came to see and I'd be pleased for you to pick me up another day, but I'll be on my way now."

"I'll drive you back," Jocelyn offered, running her hands under the tap and lifting up the towel. Thorfinn opened his mouth to protest but Mrs. McFea forestalled him.

"I'm grateful to you, Thorfinn, and you're not a bad lad, but I'll travel home with Mrs. Fenwick. If she's going to be my neighbour, there are one or two things we need to talk about."

"I have not decided anything yet," Jocelyn said quickly, wondering what the things were that Mrs. McFea needed to discuss.

"Ah, well, the house will still be there when you do decide."

Jocelyn looked back at Hanna and Thorfinn over her shoulder, hiding a wry smile from her companion, and saying: "I won't be too long."

She let Mrs. McFea take her arm and they started to walk slowly over the muddy ruts in the courtyard.

"I'll just take a look in the barn first," Mrs. McFea said, veering off in that direction. They could hear raucous music emanating from a radio inside, and they found Mike and Pete cementing up the edges of the large picture window that had been knocked out at the end. Once it was glazed, it would give a magnificent panoramic view over the bay.

"My, my, what a change," Mrs. McFea commented, peering in. Her voice alerted the two men to visitors and Mike immediately put down his trowel, taking no notice of her plea not to let her interrupt their work.

"You'll be wanting to know where we found the skeleton," he began, turning off the radio and sauntering towards her.

"That was not my reason for looking in," Mrs. McFea responded smartly, but Mike was not fooled and told her anyway. When he had finished his much-repeated story, adding a few grisly embellishments, she said: "I played in here when I was a bairn, you know. I just wanted to see the place again."

"Not much left to see."

"But it brings back memories. I remember the hay being gated off to our left here and the horse was stalled right down that end."

"Down where we found the body?"

"No, there was a tap on that end wall, fed from the water tank outside and, I think, a grain box too." She nodded to Pete who had wandered up to join them, a cigarette dangling from his mouth. "The horse's collar and tack hung on the wall here with all sorts of other bits and pieces on shelves."

"Did they hae a horse?" Pete asked. "I wouldna have thocht they were that sort."

"A working horse. A great big Clydesdale it was. My uncle used to lift me up on to its back sometimes." Mrs. McFea smiled in reminiscence. "It was a long way down from up there."

"I bet."

"The plough and the harvester were over there and the cart was tipped up against that wall in the winter."

"You've a grand memory," Mike flattered, adding: "The place was full of junk when we got here. The tractor was as old as they come, and the other farm machinery was rusty and obsolete."

"I'm not surprised. There's not much money in farming these days," Mrs. McFea said matter-of-factly and they agreed. There were not many people on Trowsay who did not have a connection with farming, in one way or another. "Ah, well that's how it goes." She turned away, taking Jocelyn's arm again. "It's time you were back at your work or Mrs. Treatham will be after me," was her parting shot, but it did not find its mark. The men stayed where they were.

Jocelyn was particularly attentive in settling Mrs. McFea into her front seat and helping to attach her seat belt, not wanting to be reprimanded for inconsiderate behaviour.

"Thank you, lass. I'm right glad you offered to take me back. I'm too tired to be doing with Thorfinn's silly ways." She lay back against the headrest, watching Jocelyn get in and start the engine. "I'm not used to this sort of excitement," she went on, giving the two men standing in the barn door a brief wave of farewell. "I can't think what Callum will say when I tell him what I've been up to this morning......"

Jocelyn let her talk, murmuring the occasional sympathetic word or interested question, as she drove along the straight tarmac road from the bottom of the Selkie Bay farm track to the crossing. From a distance, she could see Davey sitting on a grassy hummock waiting. He got to his feet when he saw her coming and Heidi responded by running hither and thither across the road, forcing her to slow down and then stop.

"There you are then, Davey," Mrs. McFea greeted him as her window slid down. "How have you been?"

"There's nothing wrong with me," Davey told her, adding morosely. "That nurse from over by was in this morning, doing this and that. Kept me at home it did."

"We wondered where you were," Mrs. McFea said, flicking her hand at Heidi who was jumping up and scratching at the door panel with her claws. Mrs. McFea had been accustomed to a variety of gun dogs traipsing in and out of the Trowsay House kitchen but she had never cared for them and Davey was told to keep his dog in check. On a gentle word of command, Heidi lay down on the verge, but as soon as her master's attention was redirected, she slunk round to Jocelyn's side of the car, hoping for a more affectionate response to her welcome.

"Are they all fine up at Brawtoon?"

"Aye, as far as I can tell," was Davey's canny response. "I haven't called in today yet." He bent down to greet Jocelyn before enquiring about Callum's health.

"As well as can be expected."

"I hear he's efter retiring."

"He's thinking about it."

"He'll be missed."

"He will."

"And are they all fine across there at Selkie Bay?"

"They are."

"Is there any further news about that skeleton?"

"There is and there isn't," Mrs. McFea said enigmatically. "I was called across to the police station this morning."

"Why that?" Davey asked, straightening in astonishment.

Mrs. McFea opened her handbag and showed him her ring, relating the story behind its loss and discovery.

"Well, I never!" Davey exclaimed, looking back along the road as another car drew up behind them. The driver waited patiently for them to finish their conversation. "And you say it was found right there in the grave with the skeleton and all the stolen stuff from Trowsay House? I've never heard the like! We thocht he'd run off with his ill-gotten gains and taken the boat to Canada, one step ahead of the law."

"You knew about the burglary?"

"Aye, everyone knew. He was a bad lot that brother of the wife up at Selkie, although she didna see it that way. He was a good piece younger than her and she had brought him up; that's how the story goes anyhow." He lifted his bonnet a fraction and rubbed his forehead with the side of a dirt-ingrained thumb. "But how did he die and find himself under the floor of the barn?"

There was a small toot of the horn and Davey looked back to give Dan Grant of Brackenlea a wave. The Brackenlea and Selkie Bay farmland ran together.

"We'll never know for sure."

Davey chewed on that fact for a moment. "The Maconachie wife wouldna have done him any harm – not intentionally, like, any road. He was the only one she ever cared for. And Selkie himself was a mild man."

Mrs. McFea agreed with this assessment of her foster uncle's temperament, her chins wobbling in response to the nodding of her head. "More than likely it was an accident and they took the easy way out by burying him in their barn."

"Davey," Dan Grant called from his window. "I haven't got all day."

It was Jocelyn who responded to this plea by starting her engine.

Davey let them go but walked quickly behind her car and approached Dan's open window to pass on the news.

Thus, before many hours had passed, there was not a household on the island that did not know everything there was to know, and a good lot more besides.

16

Jocelyn felt as excited as a young girl as she showered and washed her hair, lifting her face to the hot jets of water and letting deliciously smelling bath milk trickle down her face and body. Reluctantly, she turned off the steamy water and stepped out of the cubicle, rubbing herself dry and wrapping a towel round, before making a turban of another. She opened the bathroom door cautiously, to make sure that there was no one about on the top landing, and then skipped along to her room. Once she was sitting in front of her mirror, she unwrapped the turban and combed her hair through, shaking her head to allow air and lightness to part the strands, before smoothing it into the shape of her head and pressing jagged strands into place on her cheeks and forehead. While it dried, she gave herself a proper manicure, filing and feeding, buffing and polishing, smiling to herself at the care she was taking with her appearance, after many years of being content with a scrub and a light covering of tinted face cream.

She was only half-dressed when there was a knock on her door.

"Who is it?" she called, reaching for her dressing gown.

"It's only me."

She recognised Hanna's voice and invited her in, turning to admire what she was wearing for their night out. Her praise was genuine but some of her joy evaporated. Hanna had on a filmy trouser suit with rows of multi-coloured and multi-shaped beads falling from her neck to her waist. Jocelyn's only evening outfit was the blue, patterned dress that she had worn on her first evening at Atlanticscape. She liked it and she knew that it suited her, but it seemed too conventional and staid when compared with Hanna's clothes. She knew that Bridget would also be wearing exotic finery.

"Do you mind if I stay and chat while you get ready?" Hanna asked.

"Of course not." Jocelyn stepped into her dress and pulled it up over her shoulders, wondering why Hanna had come up to see her.

"Let me," Hanna offered, going behind and pulling the back of her dress together, before zipping it up. She sat down on the bed and fiddled with the chain strap of Jocelyn's handbag.

"What is it, Hanna?"

"I've been thinking about you renting Thorfinn's cottage."

Jocelyn turned to her in surprise. "You don't sound keen on the idea. Don't you want me to take it off your hands?"

"It's between you and Thorfinn."

"No, it isn't. I wouldn't arrange anything behind your back."

"Thorfinn was left that cottage by the last owner of Trowsay House – that is before us. It is his to do with as he wants."

"I see." Jocelyn was mystified by the conversation. She could not understand why Hanna was so unenthusiastic about the possibility of her living close to them when they had become good friends over the last ten days.

"Do you really want to move away from Atlanticscape?"

"To tell you the truth, Hanna, everything is in a bit of flux at the moment." She sat back down at her dressing-table and reached for a pot of face cream. "I like it here but Phil advertised for artists and my enthusiasm for spending day after day painting has waned."

"That won't worry, Phil. You've become a friend."

"Even so...."

"I had hoped that you would still be with him, when we pack up and move over to Selkie."

"Oh, is that why you were asking about the cottage?"

"Why else?"

"I couldn't really work it out." She smiled, keeping her thoughts to herself. "How long do you think it'll be before you are ready to move in?"

"I'm not sure. Thorfinn will be going back to work on Monday which will slow things down. Probably in the middle of next month."

"I'll come back before then."

Hanna's eyes opened wide in astonishment. "Are you leaving?" she asked.

"I must go home next week to sort things out."

Hanna waited for her to go on but Jocelyn said no more. She continued with her make-up, looking at Hanna, from time to time, through the mirror. Hanna's gaze never wavered, but eventually she looked away. "Phil will be lonely when we all move on. He needs someone to look after."

"I know he does." Jocelyn finished at the dressing-table and got up. "Is that why you bought him another dog?"

"We thought it would be company for him, but he was surprisingly unenthusiastic."

"Not any longer."

"They do seem to be bonding, don't they?"

Jocelyn agreed, pushing her feet into neat, high-heeled shoes standing beneath the wardrobe. "And Bridget seems set to stay."

Hanna shrugged, lifting her hand in a dismissive gesture.

"Actually Phil told me this morning that he might sell up."

"He won't sell," Hanna said with certainty. "He just doesn't want to be left with Bridget on his own." She got up and smoothed over the bed cover. "His memories are here, and he would be hard pressed to find anywhere else large enough to take all Duncan's paintings."

Jocelyn agreed, whirling round and making the irregular shapes in the fabric of her dress blend and separate into a kaleidoscope of muted colour. "I will always be grateful to him," she confided as they moved towards the door. "Before I came here, I was unhappy and I couldn't see a way out. Now I do."

"Do you want to tell me?"

"One day, I will." She opened the door and stepped back to let Hanna pass in front of her. "But getting back to Phil, I think his idea of having an artists' retreat in these beautiful surroundings is a good one, but perhaps he should just offer holidays. Make it time limited."

Hanna put her finger to her mouth, pointing to Bridget's door, but Bridget was already downstairs in the parlour with a glass in her hand, talking earnestly to Rab; he could not have been giving her his full attention because Jocelyn heard him saying: "Ah, here they are," before Hanna had the door fully open.

Her heart lurched on seeing him. She had not remembered him as being quite so big and broad and ruddy faced; he also looked different in pressed clothes, with his unruly red hair slicked down, a strand or two escaping from control on the crown of his head.

"Sorry to be late," Hanna apologised.

"You're not late. I'm early," Rab responded gallantly, putting his glass on the mantelshelf and moving to greet them. He kissed Hanna on the cheek and squeezed Jocelyn's hand.

Jocelyn said formally: "Good evening, Rab," and he chuckled, his eyes half-closing beneath his sandy lashes and twinkling with amusement. He put his arm around her shoulders, cupping her upper arm and pulling her towards his thigh momentarily, before releasing his grip. It had an immediate effect on her metabolism.

"Oh, do you know each other?" Bridget asked, with a questioning lift to her eyebrows. She did not hide her disappointment at having Rab removed from her orbit.

"A bit," Rab responded mischievously, and Jocelyn blushed.

"Of course you've not been painting much lately, have you, Jocelyn?" Bridget went on, changing her position beside the fire so that they could form a loose circle. "I suppose you've been out exploring and getting to know the locals."

Jocelyn agreed that she had.

"She has also been helping me with the work over at Selkie," Hanna said smartly, "and it's a hard and smelly job at the moment."

Bridget asked what she was doing and the conversation dwelt on the progress being made to get the farmhouse ready for occupation and inevitably to the barn and the skeleton. Rab had heard the stories going the rounds and could even add another instalment.

"I'm told that the skull was cut and indented at the back of the head," he told them.

"Is that significant?" Hanna asked.

"Well, it suggests that it was an accident."

"Does it?"

"Injuries of that sort are generally caused by a fatal fall against the edge of something sharp and solid. Of course, in the cases I've seen, there was the additional evidence of the body being in place."

"Is the mystery solved then?"

"Only as far as it goes. There can be no certainty."

"Do you think they'll be able to identify the skeleton conclusively?"

"Perhaps."

"Davey was sure that it was Mrs. Maconachie's brother," Jocelyn pointed out, adding provocatively, with a peek up at Rab through her lashes: "What more do the police need?"

Rab threw back his head and laughed: "What more, indeed!"

"He's generally right though," Bridget murmured, when the hilarity had died down.

"He's generally wrong," Rab corrected her, "although in this case, the evidence does seem to point that way."

"If he never got to Canada," Hanna mused, "I suppose we can take it that the cousin mentioned in the will never existed."

"That certainly seems to fit the picture."

"Well, that's that then. Everything can get back to

normal. Is Thorfinn not down yet?"

"He's gone to get some water for my whisky," Rab told her.

"Let me chase it up. What would you like Jocelyn?"

"A glass of wine would be nice."

Hanna had her hand on the handle of the door when it was twisted from the other side. She stepped back to let Thorfinn come in, followed by Phil and the two boisterous dogs. Phil was very splendidly dressed in grey trousers and waistcoat with a polka-dotted, pink shirt and a floppy bow tie, unlike the other two men who wore jeans and open-necked shirts.

"Isn't this jolly," Phil said, padding over to poke the fire and straighten one of Duncan's paintings. "We're going to have a memorable evening; I feel it in my bones."

By then, they had already eaten up at Greybarns, Sweyn Jimson's home. They were sitting round the television set, watching a Saturday night show; at least Jill Jimson was watching it. Christina, her eighteen-year-old daughter, was only looking up at the screen from time to time, and the three men were dozing. When there was a joke or antic that appealed to Jill's sense of humour, she would laugh quietly, looking across at Christina, wanting to share the moment, but Christina just went on filing her nails, deep in her own thoughts.

The loud music at the end of the show blared out and Jill quickly reached for the remote control, but it was too late. Ronald opened his eyes.

"That's better," he said, straightening up in his chair and smoothing down his hair. Ronald Jimson was a dairy farmer: he was up very early in the morning for the milking and did not finish his working day until late afternoon. A catnap after meals was part of his daily routine.

The two younger men were more reluctant to wake. Sweyn's deep breathing faltered and he shifted his position but that was all; Bill's eyelids flickered but he did not seem to even reach consciousness. They had only got back to the mainland the evening before and had travelled up to Trowsay that morning; it took a day or two to unwind and make up for the gruelling routine out on the rigs.

Christina dug Sweyn in the ribs saying: "Wakey-wakey."

"Lay off."

"It's the ceilidh tonight," she reminded him, looking across at Bill.

Their voices penetrated Bill's dream and he woke up. For a moment he looked dazed, as if he didn't know exactly where he was, then he pulled himself up in his chair and apologised to Jill for falling asleep.

"You just relax now," Jill said soothingly, as Ronald lifted a large log on to the fire and adjusted its position with his foot.

"Daddy!" Christina protested, getting up. "We're going out soon."

"Right enough." He made to lift the log off on to the hearth, but Sweyn said to leave it there, as they were going to watch the match first.

Christina pouted, putting her weight on one foot and twirling a strand of hair. "Aren't you coming?" she asked, looking from him to Bill.

"Probably."

"You'll make him come, won't you, Bill."

"Don't worry," Bill said, smiling across at her.

"You would enjoy it."

Sweyn groaned.

"Now, Sweyn, stop annoying your sister," Ronald said, putting his arm across Christina's shoulder affectionately. "Off you go and get ready, lass."

"They'll come down to the dance later," Jill assured her as they moved towards the door.

Ronald said jocularly: "In fact by the time you and Jill have finished titivating, the match will probably be over."

Neither woman responded to his quip, Jill merely saying, as she was leaving the room: "Don't be too long, Ronald."

"I'll be up shortly," he assured her, offering to get some beers for the men.

"I'll get them, Dad," Sweyn said. He lifted the remote control from the arm of Jill's chair and changed the channel, before going through to the kitchen and coming back with two four-packs.

"You won't drive with that lot on board," his father cautioned.

"Naw. We'll walk down if we're coming."

"Fine that."

The Greybarns' land was bordered by Shaws on one side and the hotel's heather moorland on the other so it was not far to walk, but when the others left for the dance, the two men looked well settled, lounging in the armchairs beside a roaring fire with beer cans in their hands.

The music from The Livebeats, Trowsay's local, amateur band, was pulsating the air round Trowsay House when the two cars arrived from Atlanticscape. Phil circled the car park without success and stopped Rab on his way in.

"No spaces left," he called.

Rab backed up and they retraced their route along the main road, branching off down the track to the loch church. They found places there between cars and trucks parked at all angles along the grassy verges.

"There's a good crowd here already," Phil commented, leading the way round the church to the path that ran along the edge of the loch to the bottom terrace of the hotel.

Rab asked Jocelyn if she had been into the church.

"I've been to the services on Sunday mornings."

"Ah, a religiose," he smiled, taking her hand as they started to follow the others.

"Not especially. I just came here my first Sunday and kept coming back."

"It's a fascinating building, isn't it," Rab commented, stopping and looking back. The church was in a traditional Celtic cross design with a simple bell tower.

Jocelyn agreed, adding: "I love the window." A plate glass window in the wall overlooking the loch showed the etched silhouette of two of the disciples casting their nets. "In fact, my mind was apt to wander during the sermon. There were nearly always fishermen out there, drifting up and down."

"Poor Miss Silver. She can't compete,"

"It made me think though."

"In what way?"

"The symbolism of it. Besides the etching itself, the clear pane of glass brings the outside inside and visa versa, uniting the secular with the religious."

"That's a bit deep for me. I'll have to think about it." They started walking in single file along the narrow, well-trodden path at the edge of the loch, the water lapping gently against the shore. "I was married there," Rab said softly, putting his hands on her shoulders. "You don't mind me talking about Ursula, do you?"

"Of course not. If you didn't talk about her, there would always be an awkward shadow between us."

They reached the path below the terraces and he came up beside her, taking her hand and squeezing it, as they started to climb the two flights of steps leading to the hotel forecourt. At the first level, he took her in his arms. "But love does strike twice," he whispered into her hair.

"For me too."

He held her away from him, looking deeply into her eyes for verification, before swinging her off her feet in a twirl of exuberant joy.

"Come on you two," Thorfinn called from above. "Less dilly-dallying down there."

Bridget had gone ahead with Phil and was waiting for them under the portico so that she could point out the stained glass window that she had created.

"It is truly lovely, Bridget," Jocelyn said, fingering the glass between the lead struts, the colours glowing in the light from behind. She thought it was an abstract design but when she stood back, she began to see different features, sometimes melding together and occasionally interlocking, so that shimmering water or rippling meadow contained the shape of a bird, a tree or a fish. "You've got real talent."

Bridget smiled with pride and pleasure. "I've carried the same theme into my drawings for the replacement window over here," she said, taking them to the other side of the front door to witness where it would be installed.

"Good for you."

"It takes a lot of time to work it all out and finalise the design, so I hope they will agree to the commission."

"I'm sure they will," Jocelyn responded kindly, glancing surreptitiously in Hanna's direction and noting her wry smile. Bridget was not going to be shifted from Atlanticscape very easily.

"Would you like a drink?" Thorfinn asked, as they crossed the hall and passed the cocktail lounge.

"Let's find a table and see what's going on first," Phil said, nearly walking into Hanna who had stopped to survey the parquet flooring. It was showing the wear and tear of many feet passing through.

"What a mess!"

"It's not kept as well as it was in your day."

"It certainly isn't."

"Never mind, my lovely. It's not your palaver," Thorfinn consoled, putting his arm around her waist, as they walked along the corridor to the ballroom in the jutting wing of the Victorian mansion.

They joined the dancers in the middle of a medley and when the music stopped, they changed partners. Jocelyn parted from Rab, and found herself looking down into the upturned face of a child who was little more than six. She took his hands and tried to match her steps to his small strides as they walked and circled their way round. With the next change of partner, she met an elderly stranger who took the dance seriously and did not speak a word to her, only making the semblance of a bow when they parted. Before the final chord ending the dance, she was first partnered with a matronly woman who did not introduce herself but knew all about Jocelyn, and then a youth who moved in his own intricate and loose-limbed way, which she tried unsuccessfully to match. As Phil had said, it was truly a family affair.

They all joined up again at a table in the far corner, changing partners for the next dance, a highland schottische, which left them breathless. Thorfinn went off to the bar to get some drinks to revive them and Jocelyn was immediately approached by a red-faced, corpulent farmer who seemed hopeful of prising her away from Rab. Rab knew who he was and sat back with a foot on the rim of the chair she had vacated, watching her, as she progressed round the room. Her partner did not immediately return her to her table, taking her to introduce her to his extended family, and she found herself with another partner. But Rab got up when they were dancing near to him and she was delivered back with a good-natured shrug. Everyone knew that he had staked a claim, although the right of trespass at a social occasion was accepted. At the interval, while the band was having a liquid break, there were impromptu songs and recitations in dialect, which Jocelyn barely understood, but she laughed along with the rest.

"Did you understand any of that?" she asked Rab as he whirled her back on to the floor.

"Not a word."

They looked up into each other's smiling eyes and

Rab pulled her closer into his arms. They were moving to the dance music as one until Jocelyn circled round in the middle of the floor and came face to face with Bill. He had no partner and had obviously crossed the room to stop her in her tracks.

"Bill!" she gasped, her heart starting to pound. "Where did you spring from?"

He said nothing. He just looked at her, his body taut and his face white with anger.

Rab said quietly: "Come on, let's get away from here," and guided Jocelyn to the edge of the dance floor. She turned to face Bill, very conscious that everyone in the room was aware of the drama taking place in their midst. She could see Phil getting up and hastening towards them.

It took Bill a few seconds to find his tongue. "So what have you got to say for yourself, Jo?" he asked aggressively.

"Leave it off, mate."

"You keep out of it."

"It's all right, Rab."

"No, it's not all right."

"Bill, stop it! You can't make a scene here."

Phil lumbered up beside her, breathing heavily "What's wrong?" he asked in bewilderment.

"What's wrong," Bill rejoined, repeating the words with rising impetus. "You ask this two-timing liar here, what's wrong?"

"Stop that!" Rab advised authoritatively, putting a hand on Bill's arm.

"Go to hell," he retorted, throwing Rab's hand off and starting to zigzag his way through the moving dancers towards the door.

Rab watched him for a moment, before putting an

arm around Jocelyn and asking if she was all right.

She was rooted to the spot and could only nod.

"I should follow him," Rab went on, gazing over the heads of the dancers. Jocelyn glanced up, wanting to gauge his reaction to Bill's appearance and their emotive exchange of words. He did not show any embarrassment, only concern for her.

"Would you do that for me?" she asked in awe.

"Of course." He smiled down at her, touching her cheek with affection. "Will you be all right with Phil until I get back?"

Before she could reply, Phil was assuring Rab that he would look after her and she felt him taking her elbow and propelling her back to their corner below the dais where the band played. The musicians' eyes swivelled in their direction briefly, but there was no break in the rhythm of the music.

"Do you want to tell me?" Phil asked gently, after a period of silence.

Jocelyn's eyes filled with tears; they were about to overflow and he offered her his clean, perfectly ironed and pressed handkerchief.

"That was my step-son," Jocelyn told him, dabbing at her eyes with his handkerchief and leaving patches of black mascara.

"I see," Phil responded, his voice intimating that he did not see at all. "But why was he so angry with you?"

"I left home without telling him where I was going."

"Why?"

"I had to get away."

Phil said nothing. It was clear to Jocelyn that he was not going to probe her any further.

"He wanted us to become lovers again," she told him.

"What!"

"Bill was my boyfriend before I met his father."

Phil drew back from her, his misty grey eyes wide with incredulity and his furrowed brow deeply etched. She had known that he would be shocked but with Bill appearing and voicing his bitterness, she had to tell him.

"We had broken up nearly two years before I met Jim," Jocelyn hurried on. "You can see how Bill can be sometimes." She gave Phil his handkerchief back and he slipped it into his trouser pocket. "And it never entered my head that Jim was his father. I knew that he had a son working on oil rigs in different parts of the world but that meant nothing to me. Bill was at college when we met and had our affair."

"Fenwick is an unusual surname."

"His parents weren't married. He has his mother's maiden name."

"I see."

"Illegitimate children took their mother's name in those days."

She was so taken up with her own thoughts, it took her a moment or two to realise that Phil's silence was significant. "But it was different for her, Phil," she assured him. "Not like your mother. Mrs.Thoms met someone else and Bill has a half-brother and sister."

"Did you meet his mother?"

"I met them all. Bill only ever took me to his mother's house. He never talked about his father."

"I see," Phil said again, his jowls quivering with contained emotion

She could tell that he was finding her revelations

hard to accept but she was impelled to try and make him understand that she was the victim of circumstance and not 'a two-timer' as Bill had maintained.

"Jim asked Bill to be one of the witnesses to our marriage," she went on. "He refused but he was there in the street when we came out of the Registry Office. You can imagine the scene when he saw me."

"Were there a lot of guests?"

"Thankfully no. Only my mother and a friend."

"Well, now, that was a blessing."

"It didn't seem so at the time."

"I must ask you something," Phil said, glancing down so that she could not see the expression in his eyes. "Has Jim passed on? Are you a widow?"

"Oh, Phil, whatever can you have been thinking? Of course I am a widow. I wouldn't tell you a lie. I would never lie to you."

He seemed to buck up on hearing that, lifting his hand to acknowledge Hanna as she passed close to them, dancing with a tall stranger. Hanna was looking at Jocelyn and mouthing "OK", as a question. Jocelyn responded with a weak smile, which Hanna acknowledged over her partner's shoulder, before she was whirled away.

"We all have our troubles," Phil said, watching Hanna out of sight.

"I feel bad about accepting your hospitality for so long without saying anything," Jocelyn persisted, not able to let it go.

"There's no need to feel bad. I did not encourage confidences."

Bridget approached and would have stopped but she was swung quickly past them by her partner, a young man in tight jeans and a riskily annotated t-shirt. Jocelyn saw him winking at a group of young men lounging against the back wall, which led her to guess that Bridget's exotic appearance had led to a dare.

"Thank you, Phil."

"For what?"

"For your understanding."

Phil shrugged that off. "I hope your marriage was happy despite everything."

"Yes, it was, that is up until the….." Her mind slid away from saying the words that would bring everything back. "Jim loved me."

"I'm glad."

"He was a kind man and I needed to be cherished at that particular time, but I know now that to love someone because they love you is not right. It is a form of self-love."

Phil considered that before saying quietly: "Some people are fulfilled by bringing happiness to others."

"Like you," Jocelyn responded softly. "You are a giver rather than a taker."

"You cannot divide people into rigid categories, Jocelyn," Phil responded severely. "In close relationships, people give themselves in their own way."

"I suppose."

They both looked at the dancing, absorbed with their own thoughts. Cissie danced past with Ted, their eyes lowered, but Jocelyn felt sure that Cissie's ears would be alert for any scrap of conversation that could lead to speculation and onwards to questionable certainty.

"And Bill?" Phil asked. "Did he accept your relationship in the end?"

"Not really. Jim would meet him from time to time but, on the few occasions that we met, I could feel his contempt."

"Yet he's part of your life now."

"He came to the funeral and then started coming to see me. I had always thought that he didn't get on with his father, but I found that his relationship with him was more complex than that."

"It often is."

"He was genuinely upset."

"Understandable."

"But I hadn't expected it to affect him so deeply."

"No doubt it was guilt as well as sorrow."

Jocelyn agreed, adding: "He saw to all the awful things that needed done during the following weeks and months. I was not thinking very clearly at that time. Then he started staying over, and I didn't have the strength to object when he moved in during one of his shore leaves."

Phil tut-tutted. "That was not wise, given the circumstances."

"What could I do? I couldn't put him out. He'd seldom stayed with his father but he still had a room in the house."

Phil got up, putting his hand out to her. "Come on, let's dance our way to the door. The least we can do is make Bill feel welcome." Phil was not a good dancer but she matched her steps to his lolloping strides. "I knew there was something odd in your background," he said as they made their way round the dance floor. "Why, else, would you arrive on my doorstep without any explanation?"

"It's even odder than you think," she whispered into his shoulder.

Bill had run along the corridor and across the hall, seeing nothing, his vision blurred with rage. The cold air outside brought him up short. He walked to the edge of the top terrace and looked out across the black, glassy surface of the loch, the slither of moon barely touching it with light.

"The bitch," he said out loud, reaching into his pocket for his packet of cigarettes, unable to get over finding Jo, let alone seeing her dancing around in the arms of another man, obviously her lover. He lit his cigarette, not turning when he heard the crunch of footsteps on the gravel behind him. He thought it was Jo, hurrying to ask his forgiveness, and did not turn round.

"I'm sorry," Rab said, his voice low. "Jocelyn was wrong not to leave a message for you, but she was stressed at the time."

"Why would she be stressed?" Bill responded belligerently, surprised and disappointed not to find Jo beside him.

"I think you know."

"Know what?"

"She has told me what happened between you."

Bill took a long drag of his cigarette and then said viciously: "Did she also tell you that she killed my father?" He felt a momentary glow of triumph when there was no immediate reply. He could feel the tension in the man beside him and thought his barb had found its mark, but he was mistaken.

"She also killed her small son," Rab said quietly.

Bill turned his head away deflated. He could feel the accusation in the man's voice and did not want to face him.

Rab waited silently, unfazed.

"It was an accident," Bill mumbled eventually.

"Of course it was an accident."

"You seem to know all about everything," Bill sneered, finishing his cigarette and throwing it away.

"She still lives it."

"So you're living together, are you?"

"That's not what I said."

"I know fine what you said and I know fine what Jo has gone through. I was with her, remember."

"Tell me."

"Tell you what? The whole freaky sequence of events?"

"I know that she was walking up a cliff path from the beach when a rock fell from an overhang and propelled her into your father with fatal consequences."

"That's what happened right enough but it's only the half of it."

"There's something that she can't speak about because it is too painful. Something about her baby."

Bill turned away. He didn't want to become pally with the man beside him; knowledge gave him power over him.

"You don't need to tell me if you don't want to," Rab said, as though he had read his thoughts. "I just felt that it would be better to hear it from you."

Bill stayed stubbornly silent, but the vivid picture of his father and half-brother's deaths, and Jo's agony during the weeks that followed, had been brought back to him. "I don't want to talk about it," he murmured.

"I can understand."

"You understand nothing."

"You loved your father."

"Get lost." The beer that Bill had drunk at Greybarns, and the top up in the hotel bar before going along to the ballroom, was now making him feel maudlin. He was remembering his father's kindness and generosity and the fact that he had given nothing in return. "My Mum never had a good word to say for him."

"And the baby?"

"She never saw the baby."

"But you did?"

Bill shrugged.

"What happened?"

"Do you really want to know?" He searched in his pocket for his packet of cigarettes and, finding it empty, stuffed the packet back in his pocket. "Have you a fag?"

Rab said he didn't smoke.

"Typical," Bill scoffed, slouching down and keeping his eyes fixed on the loch ahead. "Baby James was in his papoose on my Dad's back and he cried out only once before he was crushed over and over again on the jagged rock face as my Dad somersaulted down."

The silence between them was palpable.

"That's what the man at the inquest said happened anyway. He had been following them up the cliff path and had saved Jo from falling over the edge but she had been unconscious. She only heard the details at the inquest."

"Were you with her at the inquest?"

Bill nodded, adding with renewed belligerence. "Have you had your fill now?"

Rab put his arm across Bill's shoulder in sympathy. "It's best not to dwell on it," he advised.

"Up yours," Bill said, moving away.

"We can be friends, you know."

"Not likely. Jo is my girl."

"I don't think so, Bill."

"What right have you to come poking your nose into our affair."

"It was never your affair. Jocelyn is a free spirit and you can't make her your girl by force."

The last two words sunk in and made the heat of shame rise in Bill's body. Shame for what he had tried to do and shame that this man knew about it. "I'm going back to the farm," he said, starting to walk away.

Rab put his hand on his arm. "Let the past go, Bill. It is better to come back inside, so that you and Jocelyn can make up."

"Jo. She's called Jo," Bill said angrily, shrugging Rab's hand off.

He walked away, increasing his speed when he saw Jo coming out of the front door accompanied by the large, middle-aged man he had seen earlier.

"Bill, stop!" she cried, running after him. "Please, stop, and let me speak to you." He stopped abruptly and she came round in front of him, forcing him to look at her. "Listen to me, Bill," she said intensely. "I'm sorry that I left no word but it was all too much for me. Every night and every morning I thought about your father and James, especially James, and well....you know.... that was the final straw." Bill was about to speak but she forestalled him. "I know that you wouldn't have raped me but the fact that you thought I would respond, made something snap in my head. I wanted to get away, live somewhere else, and block the past out." She took his hand and lifted it to her cheek. "I cannot return your love in the way that you want, Bill, but I am fond of you. Our shared memories are worth something, aren't they? Don't throw that away."

Jo was still holding his hand to her cheek and his resistance evaporated. He felt the tears starting to come, tears of self-pity as much as remorse, but he stemmed their flow.

"I thought you were dead," he said, his voice shaking. "At least I thought you were dead until I found out that your Mum had died over a year ago. I suppose you've been coming up here to be with that man."

"No, it isn't like that," Jo insisted, letting their linked hands drop. "This is my first time here."

Bill looked sceptical and she told him about the advertisement that she had answered.

"You're not the hippie sort," was his dismissive response. "And if you didn't come here, where did you go those other times."

"I'll let you into a secret," she whispered with a soft, mysterious smile, taking his arm and starting to lead him back towards the hotel. "Sometimes I would tell your father that I was going to visit my mother but I didn't always go."

Bill stopped walking abruptly, startled by this confession. "Did you not get on with Dad?"

"Of course I did, but it is so liberating to drop out of one's life occasionally."

"I can't believe that you would do that."

"You see you don't know everything about me," she

teased, squeezing his arm as they walked on. "I am not the saint that you think I am."

"I don't think you're a saint."

"You know what I mean."

Bill allowed himself to be guided back towards the entrance. "It was awful, sweetheart, not knowing where you were."

Jocelyn winced at his use of the endearment, but did not comment. "How did you find me?"

"I didn't find you," he said and told her about his friendship with Sweyn and his invitation to visit. "I didn't want to go back to an empty house again."

"I should have left a note."

"Yes, you should have."

"Forgive me, Bill, and let's be friends," Jocelyn begged, glancing sideways into the bar as they passed through the hall; Phil and Rab were there, looking anxious. She gave a small nod of reassurance.

"I was never just a friend, Jo. I love you."

"I know you do. But friendship is all I can offer."

The passage was thronging with people, either talking in groups or walking towards the dancing. As they passed by, some smiled at Jocelyn or lifted a hand in acknowledgement; Bill was eyed with curiosity.

"Come and dance with me," Jocelyn invited. "It's a long time since we danced together and I'd like to introduce you to my new friends."

"I've already met your red-haired oaf of a boyfriend."

Jocelyn smiled, letting that go. "You must meet the people I am staying with."

"The hippie mob?"

"You'll like them."

The introductory chords of the Pall Jones greeted them as they entered the ballroom.The circles had already formed and breaks were made for them to join the chains. Bill hung back, protesting with reluctant steps as hands gathered him in and whisked him away in one direction while Jocelyn circled in the other. She watched him as long as she could, hoping that he would stay and dance and not drop out when the music stopped. Thorfinn was coming round towards her, manipulating the rhythm of his steps so that when the music stopped, he would be opposite her; but it didn't work out like that and he was forced to move past and take his chance farther along, She found herself opposite a licked and polished Davey who swept her into his arms and manipulated her round the floor with fancy foot work. Despite his intricate movements, he could still find the breath to ask her how she came to know the man staying with the Jimsons.

She told him that Bill was her step-son.

"Is that a fact!" he exclaimed, disappointment evident in the tone of his voice. A step-son was obviously a come down, when he was expecting to hear that their relationship was more intimate. "Fancy him coming to the island without a word."

"He didn't know that I was here," Jocelyn replied slowly

"Aye, that's what I was thinking," Davey replied enigmatically. "And so, where is your man?"

"I'm a widow."

"That's what I was told at the first."

Jocelyn smiled. "It is true."

The quickstep music came to an end and Davey swung Jocelyn round in a pirouette before letting her go. "You're a grand wee dancer," were his parting words, as he moved away to join his circle again.

Jocelyn looked for Bill over the heads of the moving throng, as her hands were taken for another jog round the dance floor. She caught sight of him with Sweyn Jimson, slinking towards the door. He looked back, searching for her in the crowd, but Sweyn said something to him and he turned away. It was a relief to see him go.

When she refocused, Rab was in front of her.

"Are you all right, my love?" he asked, looking down at her anxiously.

She smiled and her expression must have told him that all was well because his face relaxed. She would have liked to have been gathered into his arms there and then but they were part of the mingling crowd on the floor.

"Come on, Rab," she heard one of the men say, taking his hand and pulling him into the circle of men. "Enough time for your canoodling later."

Their eyes met for just a moment before the band struck up the familiar music and they were off 'round the mulberry bush', but that one glance was enough for Jocelyn to be embraced in the warmth of his affection and be sure, without a doubt, that their destinies were entwined and that she would be making a home with him there on Trowsay.